# NIGHT KISSED

## CHOSEN VAMPIRE SLAYER

MILA YOUNG

JORDAN CROW

Seth had started to walk away in the direction of the house. Veronica watched him leave, and a hot spike of jealousy rammed into my chest. I grasped her chin and turned her face back to me. "Don't look at the jester in the presence of his king," I advised her curtly.

Heedless of my words, she said, "Who is that?" Her eyes flicked in Logan's general direction. "And that?"

"If you're a good girl, you might find out."

CONTENTS

# FOREWORD

I grew up watching vampire movies. Every single one I found, then I moved onto books. These tempting creatures of the night have been my weakness for so long. And it was only a matter of time that I'd finally write my own series.

What makes this series special, is that I wrote it with my husband :)

Our plan is to make this a LONG series and I can't wait for you to meet these four bigger than life characters, a new world crawling with dangerous monsters, and an enemies to lovers tale.

*If you love action packed stories with strong, sassy heroines and dominant males, you've found your next addiction.*

**Night Kissed**
**Moon Kissed**
**Blood Kissed**

**To say I'm killing it at my job is an understatement... Literally.**

Monsters. I hunt them. I kill them.

And I enjoy it, ridding the world of the vicious supernatural killers who stalk innocents and destroy lives.

Like mine. Like my family's.

That was years ago. But I'm strong now. I'm not the victim anymore. I've fought hard to become the thing they should fear—a vampire slayer. When I'm called in to investigate a chain of suspicious deaths across Alaska, I meet three of the hottest, and most dangerous, monsters I've ever seen.

Just one problem.

They're the things that go bump in the night—a vampire, a fallen angel, and a demon. Enemies I must trust with my life if I'm to solve the dark trail of mysteries before more lives are lost.

But just as hard as solving the murders is denying my attraction to them all. And as things heat up in more ways than one, I know I'll never be the same again…

That is, if I survive the evil I'm sworn to kill… and the ones I've let into my heart.

**Night Kissed is the first book in the Chosen Vampire Slayer series.**

*This is your kind of book if you love kick-ass heroines with sass to match, scorching hot monsters who take what they want, and is perfect for devourers of enemies to lovers books. Expect steam, action, and a supernatural world filled with vampires, demons, shifters, angels… and unhinged alphas who will do anything to protect their woman. Lovers of Anita Blake and True Blood, this is your next addiction.*

# PROLOGUE

## VERONICA

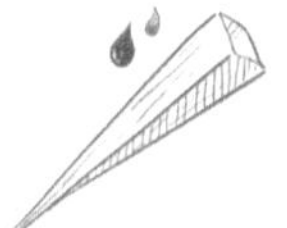

*I* realized he was staring at me. The boy with turquoise eyes, who sat two seats from me in our seventh-grade math class, who never noticed me. Why would James pay attention to a nobody in a school with two girls in beauty pageants?

But when I glanced across the snowy street in the middle of Anchorage while shopping with my parents of all people, I met his gaze. I wanted to die of humiliation that he saw me with my parents, and I quickly looked down at the old, fraying brown coat I wore.

I took in as much air as possible into my lungs, then I held it for a few seconds to slow down my racing pulse. Maybe he hadn't seen me.

I glanced up as I tripped over my own feet. Lurching forward, I felt like the biggest idiot in the world, and my cheeks flushed brutally.

"Veronica, watch where you're going," Mom reprimanded me, her voice sharp.

My father didn't say a word, but I felt his heavy stare on my back.

I flung my gaze back across the street to him. The most beautiful boy I'd ever laid eyes on was walking away, head low, no longer seeing me. My stomach knotted.

"Did you hear your mother?" Dad asked.

I nodded, but struggled to concentrate on what he said next when I kept thinking about James and if he saw me or just stared right through me.

Our car lay another few blocks away and we'd long ago left the crowds behind, when a chill swept around me. The main parking area at the shops was still closed after a man had been found butchered there over the weekend. And being close to Christmas, everyone was out shopping. Which was why we parked a million miles away. The murder got me thinking about the sheer number of killed people in our town, more than the police could explain. For the past few years, Alaska had become the state with the highest murder rate per capita as a result.

I tugged down my hat over my ears, and we moved with haste as I scanned the sidewalk behind us in case anyone followed. Mom placed her arm around me, and we hurried past closed office buildings in this area. The hairs on the back of my neck raised.

A shiver ran down my spine. It was freezing.

Finally, spotting our sedan a block away parked on the curb, we rushed forward. I wanted to get out of here and just hide in my room.

Movement from an alley we passed caught my attention.

A blur that came so suddenly, so unexpected out of the darkness that I flinched around, startled.

Three deathly pale men charged out of the alley and snatched us right off the sidewalk.

Fear iced my veins and I swallowed the terror like barbed wire.

Mom screamed; Dad twisted to punch the man. I thrashed wildly, fingers digging into another's face, crying out, "Get off me!"

A hand slapped over my mouth, shutting me up. His strength was unimaginable, the touch cold as marble.

In a blink, we were deep in the alley where the inky darkness concealed us from anyone passing along the sidewalk.

My gaze swung left and right to see where my parents were, my body shaking under the arm of my attacker. Suddenly, the man squeezed me against him, his face inches from my neck. My feet tangled, and I lost my balance as I drove my fists into his chest.

I couldn't breathe or think straight. We were trapped, stolen, and all I could remember were the news reports about the dead man in the parking area. His throat ripped out. I shook frantically, fighting the monster who watched me like a predator did prey. Dark eyes with bushy eyebrows, pale skin, a short flat nose.

An ear-piercing shriek sliced through the darkness, and I knew it was my mom. A terrifying coldness wrapped around me, numbness crawling through my limbs. I twisted my head to find her slumped on the ground, a man's mouth attached to her neck. Father lay near her, another monster on his neck, slurping, drinking his blood. Tears blurred my eyes.

Mom's eyes, wide and glassy stared at me, and

tears spilled down my cheeks, knowing her life had slipped away.

I screamed against the hand on my mouth. Rage and heartache twisted around me, shredding me to pieces.

I loathed these monsters… loathed this town… loathed myself that I couldn't save my parents.

The bastard yanked my head aside. I shoved my hands at his face, and fought with everything I had, kicking and punching, going ballistic.

The fiend grunted like an animal as he gripped one of my arms and twisted it behind my back.

Adrenaline pushed and pushed me. I felt nothing but the desperation to escape, to help my parents. My body shuddered.

With my scream, the monster bit into my neck. Sharp fangs dug into my neck, teeth sinking into me.

It hurt so badly, I cried, pummeling my fists against him, but he was a mountain. Breathing grew harder, but I still never stopped fighting.

A strange lethargy flared over me, flooding me with an unbearable exhaustion. My knees buckled out from under me instantly, but the monster held me pressed against him, slurping and licking my blood. He drew me deeper into the dark mass feathering the edges of my vision.

Crackling electricity flared down my arms, a snap of power I didn't understand. It came faster and hard, the hairs on my nape standing upright.

The vampire shoved me away so violently, I flew backward and slammed into a trash can. I collapsed on the ground, struggling to move from exhaustion.

The fiend's mouth gaped open, blood dripping out as he unleashed a horrendous screech of what sounded like pain.

I trembled, my vision fading faster and faster. The alleyway tilted around me and suddenly, my world blackened.

## CHAPTER 1

### VERONICA

**8 Years Later**

How many forensic science students could say they went to class *and* hunted vampires on the side? It wasn't really kosher to brag about that sort of thing, and yet I did take pride in it. Even if I was the only person who knew.

After a long day at college, I stood in front of the bathroom mirror and stared at the face of a girl who'd foolishly structured her schedule into dense, impenetrable walls of learning and was now paying the price. At the beginning of the semester, it had seemed like the best idea not to tempt myself with breaks between classes. Ten weeks later, it felt like walking over and over into a wall of sharp bricks.

I sighed deeply, trying to ignore the darkening circles under my eyes. After a shower, I retrieved my bag and chugged down a third of my undiluted coffee as soon as I sat in the chair at the desk. The bitterness forced some life back into my sleepy brain.

"Okay." I sucked in a deep breath. "I can totally do this."

First, I reached over to the corner of the desk and switched on my trusty police scanner. It was an older model, like a fax machine with an antenna, and it crackled as I fiddled with the dials to get a signal. It was old but affordable and that helped as money wasn't exactly streaming in when I lived off the small inheritance from my parents. But I made do with everything I had, and even worked at a local café over the Christmas season for extra money.

It only took about half a minute to pick up on a reliable signal. I'd gotten pretty good about finding the right channels. Satisfied, I turned the TV on too, just to cover my bases. The local news was in the midst of a story about the rash of graffiti "decorating" the downtown cityscape as of late.

"The police have said they can't rule out occult activity as of this report," the reporter said. She had a look of professional concern pasted onto her face.

"Well, they'd be half right," I answered.

No breaking news flashed across the television, no intrusions of sudden, horrific, and puzzling violence.

The next thing I heard was a very loud, angry buzz. I managed to trace it back down to my ringing cell phone.

I picked it up quickly, without checking the caller ID. Every fiber in my body was prepared to turn down an invitation to a night out, no matter how hard my friends ragged on me. A dozen excuses ran through my mind as I thumbed the answer button. *I'm sick. I'm studying. I accidentally microwaved a spoon and the whole thing blew up.*

"Hello?"

"Veronica? Hi, it's me."

I paused. The voice on the other end of the line

was not one I would have expected to hear at this hour. Not least because she and I were currently separated by about two thousand miles. And at least one time zone.

"Uh, hey." I leaned back in the chair and ran my fingers through the tangled nest of my hair. "What's up, Lian? Is everything okay?"

"Sorry for calling so late." Lian stifled a yawn. "We've had a really busy day, but I didn't think this could wait until morning." She paused. "Wait, let me back up and explain."

"I'd appreciate it." Despite the remnants of sleep still fogging up my brain, I was suddenly determined to stay awake. Under normal circumstances, Lian Zhao was much too polite to call anyone after midnight, including me. Even though she'd been my closest friend for the last decade of our lives. I knew something serious was up.

"Okay, listen." She paused to take a sip of something. I could see her as clearly in my mind's eye as if we were sitting across from each other: cross-legged on her bed or sofa, the phone tucked neatly between her shoulder and her ear. She was almost certainly keeping her hands busy somehow; she had to whenever she talked for longer than two minutes.

"I'm listening," I said.

"I think there's a new tribe in town." Lian had never been one to mince her words. It was one of the characteristics I loved most about her.

Now I sat up a little straighter. "What do you mean by 'tribe'?"

"Well…all right, so they've been here a while. They're bears, V. Bear shifters."

"Oh, shit." I stared absently at the channel numbers on the scanner. "How'd you find that out?"

She took a moment to reply. "Because they work for my parents. A lot of them, anyway. Let's just say I happened to witness an event one night and have kept it a secret until now."

"You saw one of them change." I chewed on my lip.

"I saw one of them change," she confirmed. "Totally didn't mean to; kind of wish I hadn't, to be honest with you. Those guys are incredibly hairy."

I chuckled. "Did he see you too?"

"Mm-mm. I don't think so." Again, she hesitated. "God, I hope not. That'd be embarrassing at best."

"I don't see the problem, then," I admitted. "Unless you just wanted to burden me with your awful confession so I'd also be haunted by the mental image of a man who looks like he's been glued to a carpet."

"No!" But I heard her grinning in spite of herself. "Shut up for a second. Look, they're working on a lot of our boats, and my dad says they really know how to haul ass. He likes them, apparently. I think they've worked out some sort of bargain."

"Uh huh. So, he knows what they are?"

"If he doesn't know directly, I think he's got to suspect they're weird in some way. All they do is hang around the boats, get smashed at the bars, and sleep. They could be cult members. But he just cares about the work ethic. You know him."

I did. Mr. Zhao was a man whose love for efficiency bordered on the fanatical. He wasn't so strict about the rules themselves, as long as things got done correctly. The fact that he wasn't bothered by a horde of extremely productive bear shifters did not surprise me at all.

"Right..." She was warming up to the point. I felt it approaching.

"The problem is, they're not very popular with anyone else. Especially not the vamp clan." Lian sighed. "There's been a huge uptick in violent crime recently. That's what I'm worried about."

I tensed. "Do you think your parents are in danger?" The notion made my blood run cold. The Zhaos were like my second family. Before losing my parents, I spent nearly every weekend at her place. We were inseparable. I couldn't live with the idea that vamps might be out to hurt them. "Are *you* in danger?"

"The shifters are super territorial and aggressive. Since their arrival, a couple of girls were found assaulted and dead locally too," Lian replied. "Then there are the vamps in the same area pissed at the bears' presence. I don't know." She shifted position, her voice waxing and waning as she moved. "It seems like they *hate* each other. Like, a lot. And right now, the vampires are winning." In the background, a keyboard clicked away. "Two bear shifter bodies have been found so far. The first one was like, last month, but the last one was two days ago."

"You can tell they're shifters?"

"Yeah. I've seen enough to recognize them by now. They're pretty obvious around the docks and in town. Not as good at blending in as the vamps tend to be." Lian let out her breath. "I'm worried, V. About a lot of things, but especially about what will happen if things keep escalating. I remember what you've told me about everything happening in Seattle, and I always thought Anchorage would be safe from that."

"I'm sorry." It was the only thing I could think to say in the moment. "What can I do to help? Name it." If she had asked me to reposition the sun, I would've died trying. That was how much this family meant to me.

"It's a lot to ask." Lian sounded sheepish. "And I'm kind of ashamed for even bringing it up, but… you're the best slayer I know."

"The only slayer you know," I corrected, smiling.

"That's not the point, smartass," she shot back. "We're like, leagues out of your jurisdiction, but I wanted to see if you could maybe come up north for a while and try to sort this out. Someone has to nip this in the bud before it spins out of control, and if anyone's going to, it'll probably be you."

I was already typing Anchorage, Alaska into the GPS on my phone. It was not a good time to take a trip, academically speaking, but I couldn't have cared less at the moment. For once in our lives, Lian needed me instead of the other way around. I was determined to be there and find out what was going on.

"This thing says it will take me forty-two hours to drive." Two days in the car wouldn't be much of a party, but again, those details were inconsequential. "Do we have that much time?"

"I mean, I hope so, but that's a hell of a drive. Let me send you a plane ticket instead."

"Come on, I can't ask you to do that," I protested.

"Oh, whatever. Mom and Dad are rich, and I'm the one asking the enormous favor of you. How soon can you leave?"

Fifteen minutes of grudging travel arrangements later, a one-way ticket to Anchorage showed up in my email inbox. A small buzz of mixed emotions surged through me to be going back to where I grew up, where I'd get to see my best friend again. I had gone back a few times since moving to Seattle after the vampire attack, and each time, my stomach churned with nerves and excitement.

I had fifteen hours to get my shit together

before takeoff. That meant packing—and figuring out what to do about school while I was gone.

"Thank you, V. I appreciate this so much."

"Don't even worry about it, seriously. But I've gotta go if I'm going to make this work. We'll talk when I get to Alaska."

"Sounds good. I'm excited to see you!"

The feeling was mutual. I could count on one hand the number of times I had actually gotten to spend time with Lian since I'd moved back to Seattle with my grandma after my parents were killed and I miraculously survived the vampire attack. Before that, Lian and I were together all the time.

I pulled my laptop over and opened up the email client, copied all my professors onto a blank message. The words flowed from my fingers as automatically as if I had planned them out for days.

"Dear Professors. I regret to inform you that I need to take an immediate leave from all classes, due to an unforeseen personal emergency…"

Outside the bedroom window, the smallest sliver of moon continued its slow sail across the darkened sky. In a matter of hours, I'd be on the train to SeaTac Airport, headed into the unknown without so much as a backward glance.

A flare of unease spiked through me... Anchorage brought back many memories that for so long I tried to push to the back of my mind. But I couldn't let that stop me from helping Lian.

SETH

Parked on a stool at the Rabbit's Foot bar, on the south side of Anchorage, I could see the blurry shapes of wet snowflakes hitting the window. I scowled. If there was one thing to complain about on the mortal plane of existence, the lousy weather occupied a place high up on my list.

But I had been promised rich rewards dependent on my ability to follow through on this mission, and I was never one to miss collecting on a debt once it was owed.

Nor did I turn down a chance to shed blood. The very thought made the edges of my mouth pull into half a smile.

The thing was, Orion, the local vampire clanmaster of Anchorage had found himself in trouble recently. The territory he'd been ruling over for decades was under threat by the vampire master from Seattle who sent over a tribe of shifters and vamps to claim the place on his behalf.

So, Orion hired me and one other guy to be the muscle and help remind these intruders the area wasn't for the taking. A brutal, violent reminder that would terrify the asshole to stay back in Seattle where he belonged.

And tonight we were rolling out the beginning of our retribution with me kicking us off. I couldn't wait.

I was ready to do what was needed to get my reward; Orion promised me my own realm in which to indulge without any rules hindering me, or others sticking their noses in my business. I had faced my fair share of shit down in the Under-world, fought to climb the hierarchy of legions, and it still got me betrayed by those closest to me. My gut churned at the thought of everything I lost...

Including her.

An ache sharpened in my chest.

Grinding my teeth, I shoved the memories

aside, loathing how they made me feel sick to my stomach.

Fuck everything and everyone. After I finished the mission with Orion, I was on my own.

As I sat back on the stool and stretched my powerfully muscled arms and shoulders, stiff from hunching for the last few hours, I glanced around the room. My mark still sat stuffed into a booth in the far corner— I could only see the edge of the man's burly right shoulder, leading down into an arm like a tree trunk. No signs of movement, let alone an intent to depart.

I resented the jackass more with every passing minute for making me wait. More than anything I wanted to march over there and finish already, but that wasn't my plan. I sighed and kept waiting for him to leave.

Twin tendrils of smoke slipped from my nostrils into air already choked by cigarette fumes. The bar was proving to be the perfect cover, in a way. Dark, hazy, full of transients and weirdos. Nobody thought twice about some guy in a long coat blowing smoke at the corner of the bar.

. . .

The whiskey had almost disappeared by the time my mark finally struggled up out of his seat. The testimony of his partial silhouette proved truthful; he was a giant of a man. A bear, one might say. I tracked the man's lumbering movement toward the door leading out into the unpleasant Alaskan night. As soon as it began to swing open, I made my long-awaited move.

The glass clunked down onto the bar, cushioned by a bill. "Keep the change," I muttered to the barkeep.

My gaze cut through the miserable, snowy night to the shadow trudging away from the Rabbit Foot's dim circle of radiance.

The hulking shadow moved slowly, weighed down by the massive quantities of alcohol percolating through his system.

When I exhaled, jets of smoke poured from my nose and leaked from the corners of my mouth. I had been instructed not to throw my strength around if I could help it.

Too bad. Showing off was one of my favorite things to do. I was always performing, whether my audience was going to live through it or not.

The mammoth stranger staggered to a halt at

the side of the road. I watched with a mix of amusement and disgust as the man bent forward, hands on his knees. He coughed and sputtered.

*Pathetic.*

I was standing within arm's reach by the time my quarry finally caught on to my presence.

"Who're you?" The words slurred from the depths of a silvered brown beard, aimed lazily over one burly shoulder. "And what the hell d'you want?"

My left hand emerged from my pocket to scratch the side of his jaw. Wreaths of steam had started to billow up from where the soles of my feet melted snow back into clear rivulets of water. I stared into the man's unfocused eyes and saw the fury smoldering there, but I'd still caught him off guard.

My right hand closed around the hilt of a long knife bearing a sharp, mean blade. If I struck true, it could puncture the heart of this giant and bring him down in seconds. On the other hand, if I was feeling exceptionally cruel…

Still sheathed inside the coat, the knife's hungry blade began to glow, first fire-orange, and then white-hot. As I drew it, the weapon lit me from beneath.

But the beast-man was undeterred. He faced me, rising to his full, impressive height. The cotton fibers of his shirt strained to contain masses of muscle beneath. "I said, what the hell do you want?" His gaze narrowed into dark slits, all traces of sickness chased away by the rush of adrenaline.

I raised the blade and its arc streaked through the night like a meteorite, drawing a trail of fire behind it. I saw a hand coming up to meet it, but his counter was far too slow.

I plunged the knife into his chest, the blade sinking into soft flesh.

Still, five huge claws raked into the flesh of my forearm, drawing a slow stream of black blood.

The stench of burning meat and hair lingered in the air, and I hissed at the second of sharpening ache before it started to heal.

The man, whose arm had morphed into a great, mauling paw from the elbow down, dropped his chin. He looked at the hilt sticking out from the left side of his chest, at the torn fabric and forest of coarse hair singeing and smoking in the heat. It was as if he didn't feel the pain at all, for a moment.

"Demon!" he snarled at me. He wasn't wrong there.

Then he let out a choking, garbled cry. It was hoarse, and it wouldn't carry far. I grinned and twisted the knife in the wound. I wrenched the knife deeper, my hand coming flush against the beast's hairy skin. I put my weight behind the blade and shoved.

The body was dead weight before it hit the ground. I glanced back at the bar, distant but not out of sight for any intruders, at the moment of impact. A tremor ran through the frozen ground. Then all was still. I glanced down at the lifeless, sprawling figure at my feet. A trickle of red ran from the parted lips into the silver-brown beard. The hand that had been a huge bear paw lay open in the snow, returned in death to its human form. Two dark eyes stared upward, glassy, unseeing.

In the end, the beast-man hadn't stood a chance. *Like always.*

I tightened my grip on the knife hilt. It was buried so deeply that for a moment, I thought it might not emerge. But then my grasp tore it free, cutting a wide swath across the upper torso.

My job was complete, and a sense of satisfaction flooded me. The vampire, Orion, who sent me on the kill reiterated that this dead bear shifter was part of the tribe trying to claim his Anchorage territory, plus had slaughtered two humans since arriving in town. More reason for him to be wiped from existence.

Five minutes later, I had slipped into the trees along the roadside, out of view of any unlucky bastard who might happen to pass by. For the moment, the kill lay shrouded in relative darkness, but the Rabbit's Foot wasn't far away. It would only be a matter of hours, if that, before the scene was discovered.

That was the vampire's intention all along. *Kill him near the bar*, he'd ordered me. *The other shifters and vamps in his tribe need to see the warning so they leave town.*

"It's done. Part one of your plan is complete," I murmured. I spoke aloud into the quiet darkness, knowing the others heard me. In answer, an impatient whisper returned on the breeze.

"What took you so long?"

I glowered at the trees around me. I recognized the vampire's maddening condescension at once. "Me? I'm not the one who picked the slowest target in this gods-forsaken city." My sudden burst of rage manifested in a quickly suppressed flash of fire. "You asked. I delivered. Come see the proof yourself."

"Fine. You're through for tonight. We'll take care of the rest."

I bristled but managed to swallow the brunt of my anger. "Don't wait up for me," I growled. The footsteps I left as I stalked off into the woods melted and ran across the crunching snow.

No reply came from the vampire. It was just as well. I had no further interest in whatever that freak had to say.

## Logan

Moments ago, Seth had announced his triumph over the bear shifter, which meant I was up to implement part two of our sordid little act to get these assholes out of Archorage. Now I stood outside Golden Klondike club, at the edge of the spread of lights out front. A larger establishment that seemed to attract supernaturals for a drink.

A whisper touched my ears. "Where are you?" The voice was mildly impatient. It belonged to Orion, the local clanmaster who'd hired me.

"I'm coming in," I answered.

Orion never responded, but it didn't matter. I already knew our time had just become limited. He'd spent weeks planning out the impending confrontation; its effectiveness hinged on the element of surprise. We weren't there to engage in a spectacle. The example had already been made of their bear shifter friend—they simply did not know it yet.

Now, it was my turn.

I slipped through the main door. An acrid haze of smoke threatened to blur my vision, mingled with the thick scents of sweat and cloying perfume.

The front room was dark and looked small, despite its size. Its main source of light were the muted lamps illuminating a handful of barely-clad women on a raised stage in the center. They rotated to hypnotic beats before a throng of admirers. Money littered the floor at their feet. I looked away.

"Not your problem, Logan," I muttered. Indeed, *my* problem occupied the circular booth in the back corner, which was stuffed to overcapacity with the club's most raucous patrons. The glint of raised glasses frequently caught my eye as I made my way closer, accompanied by loud laughter. This was the group of shifters and vampires ordered here from the Seattle clanmaster to claim Anchorage from Orion. To lay his stake, not to mention the vamp seemed to have some personal vendetta against Orion. Regardless, I was about to instigate their removal.

I stepped up to the end of their table and gradually their mean dark eyes swept over to me, six or seven sets in all.

"Can we help you?" The one who spoke smiled thinly. The very tip of a hefty fang protruded from beneath the edge of his upper lip. His arms were covered in coarse hair; tufts of it poked out from the open collar of his work shirt. In the low light, he could easily have been mistaken for some kind of bestial mutant—which is exactly what he was.

"You're making too much noise," I said.

The daggers in their gazes would have been practically lethal, were they aimed at someone prone to fear. I just stared back and grinned.

"Who're you?" The same shifter asked this question as well. He fought to keep his smile, but it was quickly curling into more of a sneer. "I can't imagine you'd do something so damn dumb on purpose, boy. You don't want to start nothin' with us tonight, I promise."

I raised an eyebrow. "Does it look like I'm playing?" A mortal man would have struggled to hear me over the awful cacophony of the music. To him, I knew my words rang clear as a bell.

He scowled deeply. Dark furrows materialized in his forehead. One hand, the fingers like a vise of flesh and bone, clenched fiercely on the edge of the table. "That was my one attempt at bein' polite," he growled. "I ain't gonna make another."

The shifter's cheeks and neck flushed a deep, searing red. A feral wildness seeped into his expression, to the point where the human shape of his body felt like a deviation, a gross mismatching of forms. I smiled at the strangeness of it all.

"Something funny, wiseass?" One of the others leapt to his feet, knocking over a glass in the process. The flood of beer doused the tablecloth, dripping in amber rivulets onto the floor. Some of the group jumped back, shouting outrage over wasted drink. I resisted the urge to roll my eyes. These creatures were nothing more than instinct and raw emotion. Heads empty of everything other than hunger, thirst, and base brutality.

How pathetic. These enemies of Orion's were neither interesting nor entertaining.

"Answer me!" This one was younger than the others at the table, more rambunctious and lithe. Before I'd even had a chance to think of a reply, he shoved his way out of the booth, sending one of his companions sprawling.

A bark of warning went up from the kid's elders. "Control yourself, boy!"

But it was too late. Blinded by inebriated rage, the boy leapt toward me, reaching with balled fists toward the front of my shirt.

He never got a chance to finish his sentence. I stepped deftly back from the side of the table. The motion unbalanced his already unsteady feet, allowing me to turn his considerable momentum against him. In one swift shift of my arm and shoulder, I condemned him to fall on the floor. He stared up at me, stunned.

"Enough!" The oldest beast had risen to his feet. His fists slammed down onto the tabletop. Silverware jumped. Another cup tipped. The club's surrounding patrons had started to turn toward the commotion, curious and judgmental. Spittle flew from the corners of the elder's mouth. "I don't have to take this shit from you!" He pointed a finger at me. "And you can bet I'm never gonna forget that ugly mug."

"Yes, you will forget," I said. "By the time I'm done with you."

The shifter's massive, meaty face went purple with fury. Using both hands, he swept up the largest, heaviest glass he could reach and hurled it at me. I dodged and heard a shriek, followed by an explosive impact.

He let out a roaring battle cry, leaping with surprising agility over his group to get to me. I grabbed him first by his shirt, breathing in the potent stench of everything he'd drunk.

"I didn't come here to start a fight," I said. That was a lie. The fight was my sole objective. "But I can finish one."

He bared his teeth. "This is about to be the worst night of your life, boy." The others were pulling in on all sides, so tightly that I couldn't see the rest of the club anymore. I welcomed the fury, the readiness to finish them. I lifted my opponent off his feet and thew him back. He staggered backward into the laden table, dropping to one knee.

The rest of his party fell on me. Punches, bites, kicks. I took it all, and the pain came and went just as fast. But I launched at them, striking them, one after the other, my hits cracking into their faces and chests. It sent them flinging backward. It all blurred into one great heap of chaos, and as messy as it grew, I started to understand why Seth loved fighting so much. The adrenaline was addictive.

I grabbed a vamp by the throat and hurled him into a bear shifter, both of them thrown off their feet.

A fist came flying toward my face. I grabbed it midair and twisted the attached arm away. I threw a vicious knee to another attacker's groin. It all would have been so much easier if I was allowed to kill them.

But no. Except for Seth's mark, Orion typically liked to reserve lethality for himself. And he had made it extremely clear that the only choice we had was to follow his egotistical whims if we wanted to see our rewards.

"Gentlemen!" The word rang out across the room, reverberating almost like a musical note. It was too late to stop the right hook I had already aimed at a vampire's face, or else I would have. The crack of my knuckles against his jaw echoed in the abrupt lull that followed Orion's interjection. We all turned.

He stood amid the wreckage of the booth

unruffled, looking as though he were floating above the torn vinyl and splintered glass in a long black coat. A fork stuck out of the seat at an angle; he pried it out and set it down. Then he looked at me. We nodded slightly at the same time. An implied passing of the baton.

Like Seth, I had done my part, messily or otherwise. Now Orion had control, just the way he wanted. I stepped back, smoothing the wrinkles out of the front of my shirt and running my fingers through my hair. No worse for the wear. All I'd lost was another night catering to Orion's whims.

In the end, a small price to pay for the spoils he had promised.

Back in heaven, I had everything. The perfect life. Friends. Future. Job. Except, I made a terrible mistake that cost me everything and got me thrown out. Each time I thought back, I kept thinking about falling literally out of the sky.

The ferocious wind tearing at my hair and wings.

My heart carved, and it took me too long to accept I'd become a fallen angel. That I was alone.

The only world I'd known had dissolved around me and my choices rapidly narrowed. I didn't have a clue how to even begin atoning for my past mistakes when I remained furious at how fast I was tossed aside.

So, I did the next best thing to survive…I had struck a deal with a vampire.

"Gentlemen." I repeated myself to make sure I had captured their attention. "Is this really necessary?" From the corner of my eye, I saw Logan do his usual disappearing act. Gone into the shadows, only to reappear at a moment's notice. Sometimes I envied him for being able to shift between the mortal realm and his.

The sharp heat of the raging inferno he had stoked was focused on me, and only me. A lesser being might have crumbled beneath the pressure, been reduced to a quivering pile of ash.

But I had been burned countless times before.

"You…" The alpha shifter glared at me through the swollen mask of bruises decorating one side of his face. Parts of his beard had been torn out, one patch clear down to the skin. There was blood in the hair; I could smell it. For all his reserve, Logan had done a decent job. "I ought to have known you were creeping around here somewhere. They told me you were a coward."

"Oh, did they?" I smiled, hiding the chill of rage that rocketed down my spine. "I'm afraid you've been misinformed."

"What the hell is going on here?" the head bouncer from the club bellowed. He was a mountain of a man who might have willingly wrestled a bear, shifter or otherwise. He grabbed two of the pack by their thickly muscled shoulders. "Actually, you know what? I don't give a rat's ass! You're out, all of you!"

It was at this point that Logan materialized again to help herd the unruly group out the front door, including their Alpha. The rest of the club patrons who hadn't already run out, stood their distance and watched us. I marched after them outside into the icy night.

I felt a little sorry for whoever ended up with the thankless task of cleaning up the mess at the club, but not sorry enough to regret a single moment. Collateral damage was a necessary, perhaps even an integral part of the way business was done in certain shadowy circles in Anchorage.

I would know. This place was my city. Mine, and no one else's. I had worked hard to keep it as mine for a long time. And I would do everything to keep it that way, and out of the hands of these intruders from Seattle.

"What kind of bullshit do you think you're pulling?" The alpha lumbered to his feet, drawing up to full height. He was taller by a significant margin, and clearly thought the difference signaled an advantage for him. He moved up into my space, deliberately casting the bulk of his shadow over the spot where I stood. "Anchorage is going to be under new management real soon. I'd pack my bags if I were you." By the time the last word left his lips, less than two feet separated us on the snowy asphalt.

"I'll paint the streets with grizzly blood before I let that happen." It took every ounce of willpower I had not to clench my fists until my knuckles hurt. "Don't ever forget who was here first."

The alpha shrugged. He grinned again. The patches of skin showing through on his chin and jaw had slowly begun to shrink as new hair grew over. His teeth lengthened. Massive, cruel claws sprouted from the tips of his fingers. The seams of his shirt swelled near to bursting.

"Someday soon," he snarled, "it'll be like you never existed." He dropped his jaw open wide and let out the beginning of a grizzly bear's primal roar. The back of his shirt ripped under the pressure of four hundred extra pounds of muscle.

"If that's a challenge, I accept." My whole body tensed in preparation for a wild fight. Behind the alpha bear, others had begun their transformations, though they were somewhat less intimidating. Shifting did nothing to counteract the effects of alcohol.

The alpha was on his hind legs, briefly silhouetted against the pale wash of moonlight spilling across the lot. One great paw arced downward toward me, claws poised to maul. I dashed in to meet him, but before I had the chance to connect, he faltered in his swing. A tortured gasp left his lungs, eyes widened, and he suddenly struggled for breath. A moment later, the shifter alpha crashed to the ground. His eyes bulged from their sockets. I watched the fur thin and gray, giving way once more to skin that now bore a sickly pallor.

"What are you doing to me?" he wheezed. The veins stood out on his neck and forehead.

At his back, his friends had scattered. There was only one figure standing behind him now. Logan's face betrayed as much as the calm surface of a lake when he withdrew his open palm from the alpha's back. Two black wings had sprouted from his shoulders, spread wide to help him channel the ethereal forces of life and death that he controlled. He'd driven his energy into the bear shifter, ripping his soul from this life and back again.

Logan's angel wings blocked out the moon, throwing us all into near pitch darkness.

I couldn't help but bristle. Hadn't he seen that I was ready to take the alpha on myself? His little show of appalling power felt like a deliberate slight, a way for him to show that no matter who was technically in charge, he had no real reason to fear me. His grin confirmed it, and my hands curled into balls.

He stepped back, melting away from my sight. My flash of anger passed as quickly as it had arrived. I knelt down to look the bear shifter in the eyes.

"Unless you want to endure that for the rest of your miserable life, I suggest you rethink who's doing the packing around here. Understand?" The hunting knife at my side sang a cold, one-note melody as I slid it from the sheath. The alpha tracked it with his unfocused gaze. "Or do you need more convincing?"

The tip of the blade found its way underneath his heavily bearded chin, slicing through the forest of silvered hair until its point found skin. The shifter's jaw clenched visibly. I prodded him, just a little. Enough to smell a fresh trickle of blood.

"You know," I said thoughtfully, "I'm sober as a mortal judge tonight. But I bet I could get a nice buzz off of you." It wasn't a joke. The pungent odor of beer lingered beneath metallic iron. I could almost taste it already.

"You're a bunch of sick freaks. All of you."

I chuckled. "Including the ones you work for."

The alpha grabbed the hilt of the knife and wrenched it away indelicately. He cut himself deeper in the process. A bright, jeweled stream of blood ran down the front of his throat, but he was undeterred. The scent of his alcohol tainted blood filled my nostrils, driving my own hunger, except I had control. My intentions had been to show those in charge back in Seattle that I wasn't taking their threat lightly and that meant leaving behind a scared tribe.

"Consider your point made," he growled. "And leave us the fuck alone."

"I'll consider my point made, and therefore expect never to see you again." I straightened up. "Or else I'm afraid things won't end so diplomatically next time."

He sneered but said nothing. His tribe had all but abandoned him for the shelter of the dark tree line at the edge of the lot. I stood my ground for as long as it took to see him shamble off into the night. Until I couldn't smell his thick, boozy blood any longer.

I did, however, smell something else. And then I heard it, the frantic sound of something running. It was too light to be a bear shifter. The lack of a beating pulse was what ultimately gave it away.

I kicked at the air, darting toward the intruder, and dragged him down to the wet earth, no more than a few feet from the end of the asphalt. Ten more yards and he might have made it to safety, but alas. I had overcome him.

"No!" He struggled feebly in my grasp. "Wait!"

"Why?" Adjusting my grip, I hauled him toward the edge of the woods. "You were there in the parking lot, weren't you? Listening to what was said?"

"Yes." He attempted to free his arm but succeeded even through dislocating his shoulder. "Ah, God!" His face scrunched up with agony.

"Then you should know I'm all out of mercy." The trees loomed before us, inescapable. He saw his fate written large upon their silent trunks. "Especially for a rat like you."

"They're coming for you," he said. "And you might think you're the big dog now, but you are nothing compared to the storm on the horizon. I guess you could call that a warning."

"Thank you," I said. "But there is no clemency for traitors."

I lashed forward, the blade in my hand biting across his chest. I made quick work of destroying his heart.

Twenty minutes later, Logan and I made our way down toward the inlet shore. I wiped the blood off my sleeve as we walked in silence.

I didn't recall everything from before I had been turned in to a vampire, but I'd grown up in a cold place with snow and storms. It was a hard life. And my father had once said, *it was better to stand and fight. By running, you'd only die tired.*

That was why I dug my heels in and had no intention of leaving my home. I'd experienced great loss, rebuilt, and lost even more. Including part of myself. That stopped now.

At the intersection in front of the Golden Klondike club, a body lay beneath the traffic light. A bear shifter. Ghastly pale, eyes wide and staring, thanks to Seth's handiwork. An example for the others to see, that they might know what retribution lay ahead. It was a warning they would never heed. I counted on their ignorance.

That was all part of the fun. My plan had been set in motion to eradicate these bastards from my territory.

# CHAPTER 4

## VERONICA

rriving at the Anchorage Grand Hotel less than twenty-four hours after Lian had called me in Seattle was a mildly surreal experience. The taxi dropped me off in front of a building whose sharp, modern angles stood in stark contrast to the rugged mountains in the background. If not for the fancy gold, '50s-era script adorning the front of its façade, I might have taken the place for a hospital or a school. Strange place, but I was too tired to complain.

The door to my room—number 502—opened to a surprisingly spacious suite of rooms. Lian had insisted upon these particular accommodations, and as soon as I saw the living room and kitchenette, I began to understand why. The drawers and cupboards had even been stocked with plates and flatware.

I called her five minutes after putting down my stuff. "Hey, it's me. Just wanted to let you know I made it."

"Great!" She laughed slightly. "You sound beat. How was the flight?"

I stifled a yawn, exhaustion raking through me. "It was fine. TSA only frisked me a little, which was nice of them."

She snorted. "It's got to be the hair. Unless you've dyed it since the last time I saw you. Again."

"Don't know what you're talking about." I ran my fingers through my hair as I talked. It had always been incredibly pale, even when I was a kid. The first time I colored it was to stop classmates from teasing me about my "grandma hair." My mom had made sure I stuck to normal colors then. Now, it was cotton-candy pink, and I kept it up because I liked it. "This is my natural color."

"Right." Lian chuckled. "Okay, go get some rest, V. We'll meet up tomorrow, but not too early. I promise."

My place in Seattle lay fifteen hundred miles south along the cold and rocky coast. Lying in Anchorage in the king-sized bed, it felt like I had stepped onto the set of a Twilight Zone episode—or maybe something just a little more sinister. The cold eye of the moon peered through a sliver in the heavy drapes. I was too tired to get up and pull them shut, but the feeling of being watched made me uneasy as I finally fell off to sleep.

Whatever was out there chased me through my dreams. A shadowy, relentless beast. Not far behind, and always gaining ground.

In the morning, I woke with my head full of fog, unable to recall anything from those dreams other than the barest feelings. My body felt like it had been filled with wet sand. By the time I was dressed and set my brush down, my phone was ringing.

"Morning," I answered without looking at the screen, secure in the knowledge that Lian was on the other end of the line.

"Hey babe. I've sent a car and there will be coffee waiting when you get here. Ten minutes. You good with that?"

"Yep, ready to go."

"See you soon!" The call ended before I could

say anything else, and I launched into preparing my backpack now devoid of my schoolbooks. I threw my laptop, a fresh notebook, some pens… and for good measure, my camera and digital recorder.

Last but not least, I grabbed my keys from the corner of the desk beneath the window. The ring wasn't large, but it was weighted down significantly by one particular item: a slender, silver shape that looked for all the world like a penlight. And it was just that, as long as you only pressed the button nestled in the rounded end.

The keys went into my jacket pocket, and I thought about them the whole way down to the lobby. That secret knife brought memories flooding back into my mind. It looked like a timeless little trinket, the kind of thing sitting at the front counter of souvenir shops. But it was actually years old, a relic of my past.

Grandma gifted it to me shortly after vampires had killed my parents. She insisted I use it to protect myself. Shortly after the attack in the alleyway, I left Anchorage to live with her in Seattle.

My chest clenched at how much I missed my parents. They didn't turn into vampires but died from being completely drained, and by some miraculous fate, I survived. It shouldn't be possible and I still didn't understand why I didn't change into one of them, why the vampire freaked out after tasting my blood.

It took me years to come to terms with losing my parents, years to embrace the new ability I'd gained from the vampire attack… a strange power to sense death and the supernatural. I still didn't fully understand why I ended up with such power, but I used it to fight the bastards. Anything to get back at what they took from me.

The vehicle that eventually pulled up in front of the hotel was an Escalade, with its windows tinted so dark they had to be illegal. I got into the back seat anyway and watched the downtown city streets roll past in muted, subdued colors. Apart from confirming my identity, the driver said not a single word. I was grateful for that.

Pulling into the long, curving driveway felt a little bit like coming home. I passed him an extra tip as I hopped from the car. With a thanks, he pulled away less than ten seconds later. I made the journey up to the wraparound porch alone, my footsteps crunching in the loose gravel of their driveway. The house was huge and rounded at the front, and the shadow it cast bathed the grass in darkness. I vividly recalled Lian's father half kneeling as he replaced the front steps in years past. Before my parents passed, I had spent just as much time here as I did at home. And being here had my stomach turning with a strange feeling. Being in Anchorage brought back heartbreaking recollections about what I'd lost, yet it also held my fondest memories from before the attack. It was a strange thing to feel both anxious and excited about a place.

"V!" The door flung open before I got the chance to reach for the bell. Lian burst out in a flurry of energy and threw her arms around me. She wore black leggings, boots, and a white puffy sleeved shirt with gold buttons down the front that suited her so perfectly. "Oh my God, it's so good to see you!" She pulled back to look me in the eye. "I can't believe you're here again."

"Honestly, neither can I." I tried to keep my voice light, but we both heard a somber tinge. The second time she hugged me, Lian squeezed hard, and I hugged her back. There was something comforting and reassuring to visit her, and when we met up , I always wished I'd done it more often.

She pulled back and studied me, grinning. "Damn, how have you been, girl? And did you dye your hair brighter, as it's super pink and super amazing. Maybe I'll get these," she flicked her short hair, "colored. Been thinking of going green." She'd cut her dark hair into an adorable pixie hairstyle, and it suited her cute face. Lips pouty and cherry red, she smiled wildly at me.

"Do it." I laughed at how adorable she looked. "How's life with you, anyway?"

She shrugged. "Okay I suppose. Dad's been getting me into the business a lot more as he wants me to get more involved in the managing side of things."

"That's exciting."

"Yeah, I guess. Anyway, let's get inside before we freeze."

I glanced indoors through the front door. "Are your parents home?"

She shook her head. "They don't even know you're here yet. I wasn't sure if you'd want me to tell them right away." She grabbed me by the hand and pulled me into the front hall. "Come on in. The coffee's all ready." And as I followed my best friend through to the enormous kitchen with the granite countertops, the tension I'd been carrying began to melt away.

"Remember that night we tried to make

popcorn and started a small fire on the stove," I mused.

Lian cut me a narrowing gaze. "Mom still reminds me of that. She didn't pay me pocket money for months."

"Which was why, I gave you half of mine." I wrapped an arm around her shoulders. "I missed you, babe."

She blew me a kiss. "I'm so excited you are back. We need to do one of our b-grade movie nights. No one will watch them with me." She pouted.

"You got yourself a deal. It's been a while since I've watched any movies. College assignments are whipping my ass."

I sat at the island, basking in the late morning sunlight pouring in from the picture windows with the idyllic view of their lawn.

She served us a cup of steaming coffee with cream, then joined me. "You're doing incredible, babe. You'll soon be one of those forensic detectives like on CSI."

"Let's see if I can pass the exams first." I laughed as I unloaded the contents of my bag and sat with my pen poised above the paper. "Okay, let's get this out of the way, then we can sit and catch up properly. So, tell me about the murders."

She beamed, but then instantly put on a serious face. Her eyes grew deadly serious. "I've never seen anything like it, V. I swear on my life." She sighed, glancing out the window. "They're butchering each other." She pushed a newspaper, a few days old, across to me. It was open to a story about the rash of violent crimes plaguing the city. The center photo depicted the edge of a local road, dirty snow banked into drifts. Swaths of dark, bloody red cut across the surface. I stared at the unmistakable imprint of a body in the snowfall.

"This doesn't look like a vamp scene," was what I told her at first. For one principal reason. "They never leave that much blood behind."

"It doesn't look like a human scene either," Lian countered.

"I don't know…" Some of my forensics books would have disagreed. "Even good old mortal men can do some serious damage to each other."

But Lian would not be persuaded otherwise. "I think they must be beefing pretty hard," she said. "Otherwise, why kill like *that*? Doesn't it seem like someone's trying to send a message?"

I couldn't hide the skepticism in my voice or

face. "I mean, I guess so." My gut told me her vamp assumption might not be completely correct. I knew that she was worried, and Lian was my best friend. "Listen, I can't promise I'll find anything out. But you need me, and I'll try to figure out what the hell is going on."

Instantly, she relaxed and smiled. "Oh, thank God. I thought you were going to bail on me for a second there." She took a sip of her coffee. "To be honest, I'm more worried about the business than anything. These are my dad's employees turning up dead. No one's going to want to work with a company where everyone's on a hit list."

The point was salient. Still didn't mean the vamps were the ones behind the carnage. Nonetheless, I had already made my commitment. "All right. If you've got any leads, I'd love to hear them. It'd help to hit the ground running." I couldn't imagine Mr. Zhao's fishing empire going belly up, but the rumor mill was a powerful force, even in the city. It wouldn't do to let shady gossip spread out of control.

"Not much," Lian admitted. "Only that someone moved into one of the big houses down along the inlet recently. It's been empty for months, but apparently there's been recent traffic.

Neighbors have seen comings and goings at night."

It was only a blip on the radar, and an uncertain one at that. Still, it was the only crumb we had. "That's a start." I jotted down the address of the formerly empty house, as well as a few of the crime scene locations. "Anything else?"

Lian was quiet for a few minutes. "I really care for you, V," she said softly. "So much. And I missed the hell out of you. Please be careful out there. I want you safe so we can grow old and move to Florida together as we agreed."

I laughed lightly. "No promises," I teased.

My friend rolled her eyes, walked around the island's granite surface, and dragged me into a hug. Her breathing quickened as I knew she worried about those close to her a lot. "I'll keep my eyes peeled for more," she assured me. "Let me know if there's any other way I can help you. Money, food, whatever."

I pulled back. "Actually, you know what would be really helpful?" I grabbed my notepad and flipped it over to a clean page, then turned it toward her, offering the pen as well. "A map."

"You got it." She beamed a smile and studied the

addresses she had just given me and then began to sketch.

Collecting my cup, I sipped my hot coffee as I watched her label landmarks and streets, an odd sense of foreboding crept up into my stomach. And no matter how hard I tried, I couldn't push it back down.

# CHAPTER 5

## ORION

I had a love-hate relationship with the house on the inlet shore. It rose three stories and an attic above the beach, and if I looked out the bedroom window on the top floor, I could see the slate-gray tide glimmering under the moon. That was the nice part.

My problem lay in the company I had chosen. Once spacious, the place had become crowded with conflicting energies, always at a high simmer. Some days it seemed as though one of us might end up a cadaver on the nightly news. Were I a betting man, my money would have gone on the demon. Nonetheless, I held my tongue. They were necessities for the moment, inconvenient generals in a war against the fools intruding upon my stronghold.

Rageful vengeance was my constant companion. I was the one who held Anchorage in the palm of my hand, who watched this microcosm spin on its axis. No one else had the right.

And I'd prove it—in any way I needed to. Fire burned through my veins with the need to hold onto it and not be driven from my home. Plus, I detested the Seattle clanmaster. Our pasts had clashed before. He took from me someone dear long ago. For that, I would destroy everything and everyone connected to him. Then I was going for him.

My enemies were relentless and always growing in number. I'd fought to claim this land for myself long ago from another clanmaster, and there was no way I'd let another take it from me.

Hence the present predicament.

If I closed my eyes, I could feel the angel and the demon in their opposite corners of the house, one brooding and cold, the other blazing with restless fire. More than once, the thought had crossed my mind that Seth might present more of an immediate threat than anything else, with the way he flung his flames around and never shut up. On the worst nights I fantasized about destroying the whole damn house—with him inside. But he offered the strength I needed, and beneath all the raging flames, Seth dealt with his own dark history. I did my research on who I asked to join me on this mission. Seth wore his fury as armor, but I trusted him to follow through on the plan as he needed a new start. I'd been there and I understood the desperation, so even if I wanted to kill him most days, a part of me sympathized with him and wanted to aid him. Though, I'd never tell him that as he'd gloat and use it against me at every argument we had.

Suddenly there was a knocking on the door. Through the peephole, I saw a lean, whipcord-tough young man, nattily dressed in a dark suit. His comb had left tracks in his oiled hair.

We stared at each other for a moment or two after I opened the door. He was obviously waiting for me to speak first, but I had nothing to say. He reeked of the rain-soaked artificiality of Seattle, the pollution and greed of the city. I knew exactly where he had come from.

"Clanmaster Orion?" The young vampire used

the correct form of address, but he barely inclined his head, and he never broke eye contact. Rarely had I seen such flagrant disrespect from one who was little more than a toady in my eyes. An errand boy sent to do his own master's bidding.

I smiled as disingenuously as possible. "To what do I owe the pleasure?" There was something about this boy that managed to grate on every nerve. Maybe it was the way he continued to stare me full in the face, his flat, pale eyes issuing the weakest form of challenge. It was maddening that he refused to look away, and even worse, that I knew he couldn't back up any threat.

"I've come to request a negotiation on behalf of Clanmaster Steele."

Just the sound of the name made my hackles want to rise. Steele was one of the master vampires from the Seattle area. I fought to keep the lengthening fangs inside my mouth. The bare desire to forgo the thin veneer of diplomacy and give in to instinct, which was to rip him limb from limb and throw the pieces into the ocean, burned white hot just below the surface. He could see it, just as I could see how he wasn't really there to negotiate. He was just there to humiliate me.

"I'll see what I can do." Brusquely, I stepped back to allow the boy to enter. He kept his shoes on. From the moment I let him across the threshold of that house, a small voice in the back of my head told me how things were going to end. But he didn't have to know how limited his time had just become.

Neither he nor I dared to sit in the parlor with the massive fireplace taking up the center of the room. The logs in it were cold at the moment. A shame, but I supposed I could use one to beat him to death in a pinch. His emotionless eyes flicked to the heavy iron poker set sitting at the side of the hearth. Our thoughts had drifted to the same cruel place. Maybe the kid knew his destiny after all.

"Clanmaster Steele wants to...acquire your territory." If there was one thing I had to admire about this whelp, albeit grudgingly, it was his unabashed directness. He was rude and lacked decorum, but at least he didn't waste too much of my time.

I laughed. "That's very funny. How does he think he's going to make that happen?"

The young man shifted his weight from foot to foot. He was bored, annoyed, impatient. An insult to my very presence. "He's open to an act of diplomacy, but he'll take it by force if he has to."

Again, I let a smirk curve my lip. "I hope for his sake that whatever force he plans to use packs a harder punch than you."

Steele's messenger scowled. I could practically see his temper rise like the mercury in a barometer. He clenched his jaw, and then he opened his mouth. "Listen, asshole. You think you're so high and mighty, running your little Podunk backwater cult? Yeah, right. I bet my boys and I could clean you out ourselves in one night." His fists clenched at his sides, white-knuckled and tense. All of his energy had been drawn in to focus on not taking a swing at me.

"You call this a worthless place, yet Steele sent you to negotiate its takeover. Interesting." I held my ground, cool and calm. The air crackled dangerously between us. But I knew better than to be the one igniting the powder keg. Not when my opponent was so green and easily manipulated.

"I told him it was a bad move," the messenger boy spat. His flat eyes had finally lit with a baleful gleam that revealed him to be on the very edge of sanity. "I said he would only be wasting his time."

He shook his head, bewildered. "But the guy insisted."

"And you had no choice but to follow his every command, whipping boy." Frank amusement colored every word I spoke. The boy was so close to the edge, the glorious point of no return.

Then his nostrils flared, and he tipped himself over. "Shut the fuck up! I came here as a favor to Steele, not to be insulted by some two-bit mini-boss!" Unable to contain his fury any longer, he let out a frustrated roar. "That's it! I can't take this bullshit anymore. I'll just bring him your head!"

He flew at me in a rabid frenzy, a hail of rapid-fire strikes. Not intimidated, I met him with equal force, and I rushed at him, both of us clashing. I shoved my hand at his throat, hurling him across the room. But the kid was fast, and reasonably strong, but his unbridled arrogance crippled his charge. I dodged his haphazard charge and buried my fist in the pit of his stomach, so hard that I swore I could nearly feel his spine. He buckled over, gasping.

"Let it be known that I'm a merciful creature," I told him quietly, my lips close to his ear. "This is your one chance to walk away."

Seconds passed. He stood precariously on the balls of his feet, his right shoulder hunched down. The effort to keep his balance made his whole wiry body tremble. I drove my knuckles harder into the scant flesh of his abdomen. He made a strangled groaning sound.

"Steele will waste your rotten blood!" was what he choked out in response.

"That's harsh." Now we could both see the end approaching, as fast and as hard as a speeding train. Opening the hand that had punched him, I shoved the kid back hard. He stumbled, arms pinwheeling for balance. Predictably, I saw him try to grab for the poker set. It was a pure defensive reaction.

It was also too late. In the next instant, I had caught him by the face, gripping his jaw in the vise of my thumb and fingers. The nails on that hand crept upward toward his temples as they lengthened into vicious talons. This time, I put the fangs on full display.

He couldn't talk, although he did try. His hands clawed uselessly at my arm, feet scrabbling against the smooth wooden floor. I glanced down at the scuff marks left by his heels and shook my head.

The voice that left me was not the one that mortals heard. I spoke to Steele's doomed henchman in my true voice, the one that belied the depths of my age. When it touched his ears, the young vamp squirmed in terror.

"You were never a negotiator, boy." I propped his chin up on the razor-sharp tip of a claw. "No. You were a sacrifice."

His terrified eyes widened. Then I was the one grabbing a poker out of the stand, gripping it firmly in my palm. Its blunted end plunged through his chest with little fanfare. The dull light drained from his eyes. His mouth went slack. No blood whatsoever dripped from the brand-new wound.

I dropped him where I stood. Out of view of the sun's descending eye, he sprawled limply over the floorboards. Nothing but a wretched shell now, a lifeless ghoul. If I had the option of waiting until morning, he would simply be incinerated into dust and blown away. But there was no doubt he'd be missed before long. After the first outsider vamp had turned up dead in the street, they'd be keeping a close eye on the rest.

Gazing down at the body, I had to admit I felt something like a stab of regret. Not because he was dead by my hand, but because I had just created more work for myself by killing him. I grimaced, bent down, seized him by the leg, and dragged him unceremoniously toward the cellar door.

Other than the thump of the corpse on the steps, the house was quiet. I could count on Seth to be gone more often than not, but I wondered if Logan was hidden in his roost, silent and listening. The thought was only disconcerting for a moment. What could he do? We were in league with each other, all three of us. Hell, I could force them to help me take the garbage out, so to speak.

And maybe I would, if for no other reason than to remind them who was in charge.

Minutes later, I locked first the cellar door, then the front door of the house behind me. I needed to gain the upper hand against those who would come searching for him in hours, if not sooner. I needed to track their movements. And there was one place I knew the rats from Seattle loved to congregate—among the bars downtown.

The trail led me toward the run-down, unimpressive façade of a place called Inlet Drive. Neon signs flickered in the two front panes of glass as I approached. I could hear the faint strains of music coming from inside.

Then there was movement in the narrow alley on the left. All my senses went on high alert. I listened for the sound of a heartbeat, a pulse, the smell of blood pumping just beneath human skin. As a figure emerged around the side of the building, heading for the entrance, I melted back into the darkness. But I could still see her with all the intensity of a beacon, especially the strange, silvery rose glow of her hair.

And for some reason, I couldn't tear my gaze away. There was something hypnotic about the way she moved, the way her body seemed to glow in the dim light, giving off its own power. I almost wanted to call out to her before she reached for the door handle and disappeared inside. The words rose dangerously close to the top of my throat, though I refused to release them.

It didn't matter. All of a sudden, the woman's face turned in my direction. Her eyes, pale and piercing, bored straight through the night into mine with uncanny precision, as if someone had whispered my exact position in her ear. Her outstretched hand dropped to her side, the door forgotten. She turned slowly.

Our eyes remained locked. A blazing heat tore through my body as I watched this woman advance on me. The shape of her silhouette awoke something feral that had lain dormant inside for decades. All I could think about was how much I wanted her, how determined I was to have her.

It seemed like she was about to make things easy.

# CHAPTER 6

## VERONICA

No matter how many times it happened, there was always a rush, a surge of adrenaline that pushed through my veins the moment I laid eyes on a vampire. Maybe it was my inner ability at sensing death, or just the knowledge that those creeps never made anything easy. This one had tried to catch me unaware as he stared from the shadows. But I'd gotten pretty good at spotting their eyes, even from a distance.

Sometimes the vamps did their little disappearing act once they had been picked out. It was the world's most annoying party trick, the way they seemed to be able to melt back into the darkness. This time, I knew immediately that things would be different. He stood almost in the middle of the street with his shoulders back and his head held high, dressed in black pants, boots, and a long matching coat that did nothing to conceal the width of his shoulders and chest. As I approached, the air grew thick with silent tension.

The vampire did not back down. Actually, he seemed to rise up taller the closer I got, standing at six-foot-six at least. His burning, gold-ringed, silver eyes, never left my face, and I studied him, hating to admit that this blood-sucker was extremely easy on the eyes. That old saying, tall, dark and handsome was wasted on him. He was ridiculously gorgeous in a rugged, going to tear your heart out, kind of way. Well, of course, vampires were ruthless killers. Yet, he had me pause long enough to admire him, the way he stood proudly, which I rarely did. I could hear the blood pounding in my ears, which meant he heard it too. We stared at each other, both of us defiant, unwilling to give any ground.

"You're new here." He spoke softly, but the chill in his low, silky voice would've carried a hundred miles. "That's interesting."

"Or maybe you haven't been paying attention," I replied, never taking my eyes off him.

He glanced over my body, and I found myself

fighting against the ripple of a freezing shiver. What was it about his expression that needled its way so effortlessly under my skin? He looked at me like I was trash in the gutter he might choose to pick through. Like I was already dead.

But then his lips curled over into a smile. Half amusement, half annoyance, and totally infuriating. The short laugh that followed only made things worse. "Not likely, little one. There are very few who know this city as well as I do. And I'm sure I haven't seen that face before."

*I could say the same to you.* The words came within a breath of jumping out of my mouth before common sense took over. No name surfaced in my mind, but whoever stood in front of me was no run-of-the-mill grunt.

"Well," I said out loud, "are you going to introduce yourself, or should we stand here and savor the awkwardness?" For good measure, I folded my arms and shifted my weight to my back foot. He didn't seem like the typical vampire, and seeing I just arrived town, I needed to quickly work out who was who in the hierarchy of vampires. "It's up to you. I can go either way."

Once again, he appraised me. I could see the gears turning in his head, underneath waves of thick hair so dark it blended into the night. "I wouldn't normally allow someone like you to speak to me with such disrespect." The icy edge underneath each word compelled me to believe him. "But I'll forgive your ignorance—this time." The smirk returned to his lips. "I am the clanmaster of the Alaskan territory. My name is Orion." He paused. "You would do well to remember it."

I resisted the urge to roll my eyes. Most of the vamps I had met could not have pulled off a line like that without looking like corny idiots. This guy, however... He could've made the phone book sound like a death threat. I had known him for all of two minutes, and it was already way too tempting to get drawn into the sheer power of his energy. A shiver zipped down my spine at how my body reacted to him because that distracted me from focusing on who stood before me.

"All right, fine, Orion." I refused to give him the satisfaction of admitting how recently I'd arrived. "Let me just start out by saying, if you want to run me out of your town, you're in for a hell of a fight. I don't do anything quietly."

The way his eyes roamed over me was both uncomfortable and mesmerizing. It was like he had the power to see directly through me, and for the first time in my career as a slayer, I wondered if I might be in over my head. Eight years ago, I'd gained a supernatural ability that gave me an advantage against these fiends, but there was also my heightened strength I never gave too much thought to. I always wondered if that came after the vampire attack as well. That terrifying day of the attack had left me changed forever. It made me something I didn't understand. Someone stronger, more agile, and coupled with the energy to trace down death, I was a force to be reckoned with. Sure, all the research in the world gave me no insight into what I'd become after the attack, but it didn't stop me from using what I'd gained.

Yet the vibes radiating from Orion seemed different and overpowering.

The thought only lingered for a second, but it was long enough to shake me. The stake at my belt that I carried everywhere weighed heavier as a reminder it was ready to be used.

Orion chuckled. "We'll see about that." When he moved, my whole body tensed automatically, a motion he seemed to appreciate. I was ready for him to come at me, to start a fight right there in the street. In Seattle, we would have been at each other's throats already. But he surprised me by stepping backward rather than forward. "Don't get too comfortable," he warned. "I'm watching you."

The tone of his voice made my spine tingle. I was so used to vamps being vile, repulsive creatures, and Orion still was, in a way. There was no mistaking the monster lurking just behind his smooth exterior. But he was also enticing, which was a thought I had never dared to think before. Disgusted with myself, I shoved it as far away as possible.

"Do whatever you want," I said coolly. "I'm not going anywhere."

He nodded. "I know."

Then he was gone, so suddenly it felt as though he could have been a mirage. I took a deep breath and let it out slowly. The drum of my heartbeat was just beginning to slow down, and my cheeks burned hot against the cold Alaska night.

"What the hell just happened?" I muttered, shaking my head. I'd meant to spend a while in the bar, but now I wanted to get out of there. The vampire's appearance had thrown my whole night out of whack, and I couldn't shake the feeling he was still close by. With the hairs on the back of my neck standing up, I turned around and retraced my steps back to the hotel.

"Back so soon?" The night clerk glanced up from her post behind the reception desk, first at me, and then out the window. "It gets pretty cold out there at night, even this late into the spring. You'll get used to it." She had seen me leave minutes earlier.

"Yeah." I smiled sheepishly. "Thought I was ready for a night on the town, but…I decided I'd rather stay in and watch a movie."

She laughed. "I won't tell anyone."

It didn't hit me until I stood in my room three minutes later with the remote control in my hand that this jackass who called himself Orion had managed to make me into a joke without even trying. Instantly, my feelings shifted from muddled confusion to anger and resentment, as if a fog had lifted from my brain. If there was ever a time I realized how much I still had to learn, it was right in that moment.

"Shit," I whispered. The reality of the situation was that he had chased me back into the corner without taking a single step forward. And he probably knew it, too. Sighing in frustration, I raked both hands through my hair, letting it fall angrily down my back.

It was safc to assume that Orion hadn't been kidding about watching me—if he really was the regional clanmaster, he'd have eyes in a lot of places. And that meant he could pop up wherever he wanted, unannounced. I was determined not to be caught off guard again.

*Next time,* I vowed, *he won't be so lucky.*

*L*ian and I had mapped out more scenes of as many murders as she had information on, and in the days following my first encounter with Orion, I hit the pavement hard.

Most of the sites we had pinpointed, especially the older warehouses and rundown houses, were long since cleaned up or degraded, but the air still hummed with the residual energy of violence. Sometimes it was difficult to find a quiet moment away from the eyes of the city to commune with the spot, but patience and perseverance proved to be my best friends. I spent the next few days walking around in phantom worlds of blood and death, terror lingering like a memory in the fresh mountain air.

The work was haunting and draining in equal measure, and it left me chased by nightmares filled with creatures whose faces I couldn't see. But despite my best efforts, the perpetrators' identities remained unknown to me for days. If I saw any of them, it was only as silhouettes, vanishing like smoke on the wind. The thing that stuck was the power of their energies. Like Orion's, but not quite the same. His was unlike anything I had seen or felt before.

It made me certain that something bad was going down in Anchorage.

On my way back to the hotel, a shadow caught my attention from between two homes. A small passage, flanked by tall wooden fences.

When a scream tore free that direction, I sprinted toward the sound without hesitation. Fingering the stake on my belt, I retrieved it, and followed the curve of the passage. A thin layer of snow crunched under my quick steps when I happened upon two vamps cornering a young boy who hugged his school bag, shaking. Terror flooded his huge eyes when he looked my way with a pleading expression of help.

"For hell's sake," I started, lifting my stake, twirling it in my hand. "You bloodsuckers are so predictable."

The darkhaired one swept his gaze up and down my body, his attention stopping on my stake, then threw his head back with laughter. "Come over here, and I'll show you what a real weapon looks like."

I rolled my eyes at his cliché line. The second vamp sneered in my direction, nostrils flaring.

Just then the young boy slipped free and darted out of their grasp.

The fiends twisted in his direction, but I called out, "I bet you two can't take me on."

Vampires had egos to match their bloodlust, and as predicted, they both turned in my direction, leaving the boy alone.

A deep guttural sound tore from one of their throats, and with the wind growing colder, I didn't have time to tap dance with these monsters. They came at me.

Inches from their grasp, I threw myself into a low forward roll right between them.

Throwing myself to my feet, I spun around and drove the stake right into one of the fiend's back, right over the heart. He arched, his knees already buckling as he gurgled his protests.

Except, the second bastard moved faster than I expected. He tackled me and threw us both to the wet, cold ground. Stars danced behind my eyes from the impact, and I struggled to suck in a breath with his weight pressed down on my chest, laying on top of me. We were face to face, and I gagged at his putrid breath.

I shuddered as I stared into his dark eyes where only my death waited.

"Get off me," I growled, bucking against him, shoving a fist into his chest. I quickly slid my other hand down my side and grabbed my switchblade on the ring from my pocket.

"You chased away my meal," he snarled.

While I clawed at his face. His hands snatched my wrist, distracted enough as I rapidly slashed my weapon at his head.

He turned his attention to the attack, reacting a split second too slow. My blade jammed right into his eye. He flinched backward and there was a scuffle as I shoved him off me and I rolled to my feet. My heart thundered in my chest because I didn't have much time. My attack was a distraction, nothing else.

I threw myself to the first culprit, scrambling to pull the stake from his back.

A shadow fell over me.

Frantically, my fingers snatched the weapon, my muscle tightening, heaving out the stake.

I whipped around in a sliver of a second, weapon raised and swinging around toward my attacker.

Silvery eyes shone.

Lips peeled over razor-sharp fangs, his snarl echoed through the night.

No hesitation.

I plunged the stake right into his chest as he rushed into me, throwing me off my feet once more.

My lungs emptied of air, and I gasped as the dead weight slumped over me, trapping me. He gurgled over me, blood dripping into my hair.

Seconds was it all it took for such a fatal blow to a vampire to render them useless.

"Fuck!" With all my strength, I drove my palms into his shoulders, rolling him off me.

He slumped onto his back like a sack.

Up on my feet, I dusted myself of snow and used it to clean the blood out of my hair.

I stared down at the two vampires. That was

what I should have done earlier when I crossed paths with Orion, not drooled over him.

I sighed at myself as I collected my stake and took out my phone to call the cops. I would report bodies found in the alley so they were collected before anyone stumbled over them. Dead vampires once staked remain withered husks of themselves, fangs withering away and only their human body remained. Meaning discovering they were vampires was close to impossible. Sure, there would be inconsistencies in the results, but not many humans jumped to the conclusion of vamps in autopsies. So, I did my best to clean up after myself as much as possible at each fight.

I walked away, the cellphone pressed to my ear, and headed back on the street to continue my checks.

The moment I hung up from the police, my phone suddenly buzzed in my hand, and I checked to find it was Lian. She checked in with me every day, to ask about my progress and make sure I wasn't going totally insane. "How are you?" she asked, barely veiling the concern in her voice. "Find anything useful?"

Inevitably, I sighed and shook my head, even though she couldn't see me. "Not yet. All I know is, they're a different breed up here. There's got to be something in the water."

"It wasn't always like this." Lian said that a lot, and always with the same combination of morbid wonder and disbelief. "I mean it. It has gotten worse recently."

"Even more reason then, I should get back to work. Got a couple more places to visit." It wasn't a lie. She still understood my meaning perfectly.

"Right. Let me know if you need anything. I'll call if I don't hear from you."

"Thanks, Li. Love you."

"Love you too, girl. Be careful out there."

I slipped my phone into my pocket and thought about how badly I could use a long, hot shower, and a drink. For some reason, I hadn't expected my return to Anchorage to be so fraught with complicated emotions. I saw now how naïve I was being.

The last of the crime scenes I visited provided a welcome distraction. I had followed them in chronological order from least to most recent, which meant the intersection leading away from the Golden Klondike gentlemen's club practically reeked of vampire-scented brutality. A few cars cruised through as I walked along the tree line off the side of the road. As soon as I was within range, I closed my eyes and began the reconstruction.

When I opened them again, the images I saw gripped my heart in an iron fist. There was no blood to speak of, but the ghostly afterimage of the body splayed in the middle of the road was so grotesquely clear compared to most of the others. The head, twisted around on a clearly broken neck, stared blankly toward me. All of a sudden, the breath caught in my throat.

"A vampire?" That was new. The previous victims had mostly been bear shifters, just as Lian had said, but there was no mistaking the sickly pallor or the metallic irises of the corpse, clouded in death as they were. He looked a lot more like the vamps I was used to—that is to say, like he'd crawled out from under a rock.

And straight into the true embrace of death.

Another car zipped along the road, passing straight through my vision. I crouched down in the snow to get a better look across the pavement, waiting for a lull in traffic. Two more sets of headlights went by, and then the street fell dark and quiet. Now was my chance.

Springing up out of the crouch, I ran, leaping the snowbank. Exertion made the conjured images flicker, but I had long since learned how to hold my concentration on the move. The nearer I drew to the spot where the slain vamp lay, the more I could sense in the atmosphere, past energies swirling together to create an approximation of the night he died.

That was when I felt something new and all too recently familiar, the bold trace of an aura I had come across less than a week before.

Orion.

He was somewhere in the vicinity.

And another thing I recognized all mixed in, a whiff that gave me flashbacks to rain and gray skies and the clutter of a rushing cityscape pierced by the towering shape of the Space Needle.

The vamp on the ground at my feet was from Seattle. Like me, two thousand miles from home. And I was pretty sure I knew now who killed him. That piece of information shifted my focus entirely. I straightened up, lifting my head into the breeze. The remnants of the Alaskan clanmaster's energy glimmered on the breeze. Not enough time had passed to dull them beyond recognition.

I turned back toward the woods and began to follow Orion's trail.

*A* body in the cellar was something of an unwelcome surprise to both Seth and me. It had been hidden for a few days now, by the state of the corpse and the reek, once Seth had unwrapped it from the plastic casing Orion arranged. Unsurprisingly, it was another vampire, rendered ghastly pale by the uncompromising touch of Death,

Seth caught my eye as I glanced down from the top of the cellar door and motioned impatiently with one arm.

"Hey, get down here, angel-boy. We're on corpse-hauling duty tonight."

I stared at him, into fiery eyes brimming with destructive energy. He was smiling, but there was a thin mask of cruelty behind it. He was constantly on the edge of raging frenzy, waiting for any excuse to spill over. I wondered if he would come up and try to fight me.

"Where are we going?" I asked.

He shrugged, a brief, irritated jerking of the shoulders. "Orion doesn't tell me shit, the son of a bitch. He said something about throwing it into the river." The smile began to turn down into a scowl. "What are you waiting for? Get moving."

Despite knowing it would give the demon satisfaction he did not deserve, I complied. He and Orion were each too much of a hassle to deal with at their worst—the easiest thing was to keep quiet. I had nothing to prove on the surface—if a line was ever crossed, they'd find out quickly how I could hold my own.

We pulled the corpse up to ground level. Just as we dropped it on the floor, arms and legs akimbo, Orion stepped around the corner to join us.

Seth made a face. "I thought the dead ones turned to dust," he remarked.

Orion laughed mirthlessly. "In the sun, my friend, so long as the sun is the thing that does the killing. I'm afraid I've stolen the privilege for myself this time. This asshole tried to negotiate with me. Didn't turn out well for him."

Seth leaned down to lift his side of the improvised litter. "Let's get this over with. I'm already bored."

"Don't worry. When they finally realize what fate befell him, I'm certain we'll all be busy." Orion's eyes lit with a strange, almost maniacal flame every time he spoke of his rivals. I half believed he had killed this doomed creature on purpose, to goad his enemies out of dormancy. They had spent the past weeks dancing around idle, fruitless negotiations as more and more turned up mysteriously dead.

At last, it seemed that the time for halfhearted diplomacy had passed.

We walked in silent formation, the body balanced between us, through the densely forested wood between the house and the shore. The Alaskan wind blew coldly through my hair and ran its frosty fingers along my neck. To me, the sensation was a comfort, though I noticed Seth shake it away in an angry blast of steam. For once, however, he declined to speak.

We heard the river before we could see it, its voice muddied by the slough of ice rushing between its banks. The ice rumbled as it struggled for position on the ever-shifting surface.

"Here." Orion stopped. "Wait for a break in the ice."

"And what do we do if he doesn't go under?" Seth demanded. The question was on my mind as well, but I let him have the honor of asking. Judging by the way Orion's gaze narrowed slightly, it was a wise decision.

"He will." The phrase rang with finality—our leader had spoken. Seth grumbled something else under his breath. Orion turned his attention to me. "Close your eyes," he ordered. The strangeness of his command didn't strike me until I had already done as he asked. His voice, low and insidious, now sounded in the back of my mind. "Do you sense that?"

At first, no. But then I caught a foreign vibration, hiding beneath the clutter of everything else. The aura hummed in the background, quiet, unassuming. The only thing I knew initially was that it belonged to a living creature.

"Who is it?" Even as I asked it, I understood the question to be moot.

"You are about to find out." Orion steered me firmly in the direction from which the unidentified aura emanated. "Go and teach our little visitor some proper manners. And bring her back when you're finished."

I left the riverbank and headed once more into the trees. Whoever she was, she thought she was hidden. In the hush of a thickening night, I sensed her heartbeat—a little too quick. Maybe she was scared. And, well, maybe she wasn't wrong to be. As I moved among the dark trunks, she began to move in opposition. The prey could tell she had been rousted out.

This knowledge would not help her. I was nothing if not far too adept in the search for and subsequent extinguishing of life. But Orion had said to bring her back, hadn't he? That was something new and intriguing. Who was this individual, that I had not been granted the typical permission to kill on sight?

The game of cat-and-mouse went on between us for only a couple of minutes—as long as I allowed. She had nowhere to go but away from me, and I was the faster between us. Her pulse grew steadily louder in my ears, until I could nearly feel it with my own. Silent as a shadow, I rounded the trunk of the next tree…and heard a tiny gasp.

The human girl knelt on the frozen ground, staring up at me through huge, moonlike eyes. She had taken the chance to remain inconspicuous, efforts that struck me as pitiable more than anything. The dark hat over her head struggled to contain unnaturally bright waves of hair. I reached out to touch one of the escaping locks, momentarily transfixed. She made a valiant effort not to flinch.

In that moment, an impossible note of familiarity sounded within me, like the chime of a sacred bell. I looked down into her wide blue eyes and wondered if it was possible that we might have something, anything, in common.

"Who are you?" Her impressively calm inquiry shattered the spell.

"It doesn't matter." I grasped her by the arm, though not as firmly as I had meant to. She was small beneath my hands, but sturdy too. A woman of tempered glass and secret steel. And unlike the bodies I had grown so accustomed to handling, she was warm.

In a heartbeat, her free arm lashed forward, and she drove the heel of her palm into my chest, catching me off guard, which surprised me. She wrenched her other arm from my grip, and stepped back. I already liked her. She didn't let anyone push her around.

"Why not?" The girl planted her feet as hard as she could into ground. I looked into her then, at the face of her soul, the relative newness of her life. So young and vital, and yet oddly wise. Was that why Orion wanted her? I doubted it. He had never struck me as a man appreciative of depth.

"Because." I spoke in measured tones. "Ask me again, and you'll be dead." Briefly, I regretted my coarse phrasing; that type of rhetoric was usually enough to induce panic in the hearts of mortals.

She narrowed her gaze at me, her pose ready to fight me. "Fine. What do you want, then? Why are you tracking me?" The considerable weight of either courage or stupidity filling her voice was enough to give me a moment of pause. I turned halfway to see her once more. She *was* a mortal, wasn't she? The echo of that one clear note haunted me. Maybe I was misjudging her. There was something odd about her I couldn't pinpoint.

She stared at me, a cold, defiant fire now burning in her eyes. "I'm not afraid of you. If you're not going to talk, then you can be on your way."

This was partially a lie. I could feel it coming

off of her no matter how deeply she drew from her well of strength. There was nothing she could have done to mask it any further; fear was a vital instinct for any being with the inconvenient ability to die.

"Yes, you are." I leaned down. Her breath caught slightly in her throat, and she recoiled out of my reach. "Just as you should be."

She chuckled grimly. "I don't think so." The next thing I knew, she had kicked at my ribs, ripped her hat off, and thrown it in my face. The flash of black cloth was just disorienting enough to lose sight of her as she took off in the first direction she saw. I blinked and shook my head. She hadn't gotten far, what with her fragile human legs.

And now I was getting annoyed, fire igniting in my veins. As usual, the living were proving to be far more difficult than the dead. Not that it mattered, in the long run. I gave her a few seconds to believe her flight had a chance of success, and then I drew in a breath, pulling my power from the other side of the veil. The world washed white around us. I watched her slow to a halt mid-stride, her hair suspended in a glorious pink banner behind her.

My wings, no longer hidden in the liminal space between my domain and hers, weighed heavy on my back. Often, I wished they weren't necessary to use what cursed gifts I had been granted, but they were always mine to bear. They unfurled slowly as I approached her from behind. Up close, I could see her moving a fraction of an inch at a time. The sole of her right shoe descended gradually through still air. One wing formed a wall in front of the fleeing girl.

I exhaled.

She ran into a cloud of black feathers at full speed—the hollowness of my wing-bones did nothing to cushion the impact. I caught her as she reeled back, stunned.

Pivoting on the spot, she threw a fist at my shoulders and drove a knee into my gut, then shoved herself away, breaking free past my wings caging her.

She was good, but I was better.

Each wing folded against my body, and I ran after her this time, refusing to have Orion make comment regarding a human outsmarting me.

A small clearing ahead, and I spread my wings wide. They snapped outward, catching the wind and beat. My feet lifted off the ground. In seconds,

I swooped right behind her and looped my arms under her armpits, hauling her into the air.

"Put me the hell down!" She writhed against me, but I held on tight, my wings beating, carrying us over the trees. Her fingers dug into hands, pulling at my hold as she thrust for freedom.

I admired how she didn't let fear paralyze her at a time when most humans would panic.

By the time the river was back in earshot, she was kicking and shouting to be put down. I fought the sudden, vicious impulse to crush her right there, to break her delicate neck in one effortless snap. As much as I would have enjoyed it, something about her made me want to study her further, to understand who she was.

Less than a hundred feet ahead, Orion stood on the side of the water, awaiting my return. I had no doubt that if I delivered him a dead girl, she wouldn't be the only one who ended up broken. I may have held death in my hands, but as it turned out, it was harder to deal with one who was already there.

To that end, the girl was still fighting as I set her down in front of the others. Seth had just finished sending the body off downstream, and as he moved back toward us, he caught sight of the captive girl for the first time. She stumbled out of my reach, her body poised to fight. Against anyone else, she might have stood a chance.

Orion smiled. There seemed to be a hint of genuine pleasure in his expression. "Hello again, little one," he said.

The girl whipped around at the sound of his voice. From that moment on, her giant eyes never looked at anyone else.

# CHAPTER 8

## ORION

I liked the way she stared at me in that moment of true recognition, her upturned face illuminated by a fall of silver moonlight, her full lips, and cheeks rosy from the cold. Behind the mask of bravery in her blue eyes, there was a hint of fear, and also innocence. She stood about five-foot-eight, toned, and my gaze traced the curves of her full breasts. My presence had surprised her, truly. That palpable element of shock was what I enjoyed most—a way to let her know exactly where dominance lay.

"A strange place for a girl to be wandering at night in this city," I told her calmly. "Perhaps you're lost."

The vulnerable openness of her expression

instantly closed up. She seemed to age a few years as her soft mouth tightened into a straight, emotionless line and her luminous eyes hardened into stones. "I'm exactly where I planned to be." Much like she had at our first meeting, she lifted her delicate chin.

What was this pretty creature hoping to prove by pretending not to be afraid? She was no match for even quiet, brooding Logan. Had I wanted to, I could have torn the thin white skin of her throat before she had the chance to say a single word. Didn't she know she was living purely on the strength of my mercy?

Her stubborn foolhardiness elicited a grudging but genuine admiration. Seldom did I get the chance to meet mortals whose hearts and minds were able to withstand the knowledge of my nature. This human girl, on the contrary, had sought me out, followed me to my home. And now she was caught, and she still refused to back down.

"I suppose you expect me to spare you?" I spoke somewhat sternly, so that she wouldn't know I was in any way pleased to see her again.

"And I assume you'll have a price," she shot back. "How about you tell me what you three are doing out here?" Her wits were as sharp as her tongue, even under these trying circumstances. She brushed an unruly lock of wild hair from her eyes, which burned into me. Were I any weaker, that gaze might have turned my bones to ash.

"Well." I smirked. "It's very doubtful you'd have anything material that would interest me. But I think we could work something out. A payment plan, if you will." Stepping forward, I reached out to touch her face with the backs of my fingers, running my knuckles from cheekbone to jaw. She was a beautiful little thing.

A tiny shudder cracked her wall as she took a deep breath.

"I don't want to know," she said, eyeing the three of us, and the brave little thing never recoiled, "but I have a sickening feeling you're going to tell me anyway."

I laughed, unable to help it. She found a way to deepen my burgeoning fascination at every turn. Reckless, ignorant, self-endangering, and funny! How had it taken so long for this rare sort of woman to fall—almost literally—into my hands? She could not be permitted to stray too far from watchful eyes unless I wanted to risk losing her. But at the same time, I suspected she'd come back on her own even if I set her free.

After all, she had been unable to stay away once already.

The girl glanced to the side as I appraised her. When she had spoken, there were no fangs of any kind I could see, just the smooth, ineffectual even pearls of her teeth all humans carried. Yet the longer I stood so close to her, the greater I sensed something unusual, a characteristic I didn't recognize in her. Not to mention, no humans would stand before me without trembling with fear.

"Who are you, gorgeous?" For now, I kept my tone gentle and safe. Those great, jeweled eyes shifted back to mine. Her brows knit.

"Save the compliments, Romeo. My name is Veronica." She paused, holding my gaze. How fascinating seeing I haven't even tried to charm her yet. "By the way, I'm not giving you anything. Especially not what it looks like you're thinking. And you didn't answer my earlier question about what you're doing here." Veronica's whole body was tense with frigid anticipation. One hand had curled into a tight fist. On the surface, she might have seemed calm, but underneath was a cornered animal, ready to fight her way out, tooth and nail.

"We're out for a stroll." I grinned. Not discouraged, I slid my gaze over the side of her neck and over her throat. The blood pulsed through her carotid artery. I could hear it, smell it at being only a couple of feet apart. A shadow of the rich, metallic taste hovered on the surface of my tongue. My mouth began to water. But beneath that lay something new, something dangerous, something tempting. I narrowed my gaze on her. Veronica was so much more than a human. I didn't quite understand it, but a shadow lingered beneath the surface. Who exactly was she?

"Is there nothing I can do to change your mind to come home with me?"

"You have nothing I want." She held her chin high, her hands stiff by her side, and I didn't miss her gaze sweeping over the three of us constantly. She was watching our every move.

Her words had told me one thing very clearly, but the signals from her body, the heightened heartbeat, the faintest hint of red shaded her cheeks said something else entirely. "It would be a damn shame to waste a body with so much potential."

"I'm not here for your entertainment." Veronica's face reflected disgust and disdain at the same time her pulse sped up.

I knew that I had her in the palm of my hand,

no matter how hard a fight she thought she was putting up. Not to mention that all together, we had her outnumbered and outclassed.

"Then what do you want? To spy on us?"

She gave no response, but the truth showed itself at the corner of her mouth, curling upward ever so slightly. The fire was back in her eyes as she stared daggers, first at me, Seth, then at Logan. Ever dispassionate, they gazed back at her.

"I could have you killed," I replied.

"For crossing paths with you out here?" She pursed her lips in a mocking expression looking like she might break out laughing.

"You *should* just do it." Seth spoke up at last, pushing his way into our sphere. He stood at my shoulder and glowered down at the captive. Smoke rose from his nostrils, wreathing around his face. "What a waste of time. Bring her home, or let's chuck her in there too." On the last word, he jerked his thumb over his shoulder toward the icy river thundering along at his back. I glanced at the surface of the water just in time to see the last of a pale, slightly mottled hand disappear below the current.

"Enough," I warned.

The demon grunted and fell silent, but I

noticed that he, too, was transfixed by her sensuous beauty. His expression betrayed the naked lust I felt stirring within me. To see him want her so openly enraged me.

That was the moment I decided that I wanted to make her mine—in body and in spirit. Turning new vampires was a practice I had abandoned for decades, that I had, in fact, sworn never to repeat. Mistakes had been made in my careless youth, and they had cost me dearly. On the rare occasions I allowed my mind to venture back to those days, I remembered little more than brokenness and shadow, a constant crisis of faith.

One look at Veronica and those long-held convictions flew out the window. All I could think about was how she'd taste and the feeling of her death and rebirth in my arms. So many times it had been orgasmic in its own way. Pleasure mingling with pain. The thought of experiencing that moment with her filled me with a fiery passion I hadn't felt in years.

Her hand fell to her waist, which I assumed was where she kept a weapon. No one would come alone after us without a plan for when things turned bad. She took several steps backward, aware this wasn't a fight she'd win if she started one. But it occurred to me that her intention hadn't been about battling us but to gain intelligence.

The urge to sweep her up and spirit her away to the house threatened to blind me to everything else in the world. It was tempting just to say that nothing else was of consequence until I'd gotten my fill of her. But not even her potent allure erased the gravity of other, more pressing issues. My body longed to have its mounting hunger sated by her flesh, and yet I understood that she was no more than a distraction. To acquire her would be to acquire a weak point for my enemies to exploit.

That sobering reality was just enough to snap me out of the dream into which I had fallen. I realized I had been holding Veronica's face as a scholar might hold a sacred relic. Interestingly, she had let me, though the fist persisted at her side. Would she fight if we gave her cause? The prospect of putting her body through its paces threatened to pull me away into fantasy.

"If you aren't going to be forthcoming with me, I will be on my way," she said as Seth started to walk away in the direction of the house. Veronica watched him leave, and a hot spike of jealousy rammed into my chest. I grasped her chin and turned her face back to me. "Don't look at the jester in the presence of his king," I advised her curtly.

Heedless of my words and shoving my hand away, she said, "Who is that?" Her eyes flicked in Logan's general direction. "And that?"

"If you're a good girl, you might find out." The tide of my emotions rose so sharply and unexpectedly, that I struggled to contain them.

"And watch who you're manhandling, clanmaster." If my tone had been short, hers was as thin and taut as piano wire. "I promise you are underestimating me."

"Rich words from a woman who refuses to prove it," I answered quietly.

Her fear was momentarily overshadowed by anger and heat. She was angry too, and curious. Her desires were far less bold than mine, but they were rooted and growing.

I didn't want to turn her loose. It crossed my mind that the cellar was newly vacated of its unfortunate last tenant. She could take up residence there just as easily. The most immediate and complex problem was whether or not she could be convinced to stay put.

And if she was down there, I could count on

being driven to distraction every minute by the physical craving gnawing at my insides. It was useless to deny that she held a strange and unforgiving power over me, just by virtue of being a woman capable of catching and holding my attention. My desire was to spend every moment with her, picking her apart, deciphering how and why she'd managed to take up residence in my mind so quickly. And then I ached to devour her until there was no doubt left that she belonged to me.

All of which made Veronica an incredible liability. Though it pained me to admit, there was no way in hell to bring her to the house without compromising everything.

Veronica stepped farther away and looked at me, saying, "Listen, Orion. As much as I appreciate this oh so magnanimous gesture, let's get one thing straight, okay? I don't owe you for this, no matter how much you want me to. You made your choice to not hurt me. Now we're both going to have to deal with the consequences."

The grain of truth in her words stung a little. Precious little had stopped me from flinging her over my shoulder and locking her in the cellar, but I was allowing her to roam free. Maybe it was because I knew in my soul that she wouldn't wander far, that she'd keep returning of her own accord. Even then, perhaps I sensed that the fascination was mutual.

Also, it certainly helped that she wanted to destroy me. I chose not to tell her what a vain aspiration it was. The long span of my life had thus far been marred by countless dangers. One beautiful and eminently fragile human girl posed no threat.

In order to make sure she knew it, I closed the distance she'd put between us and locked an arm around her waist. Her hands braced against my chest to no avail. This time, I leaned down so close that my lips brushed her skin under her earlobe. "I'm not a man to whom consequences normally apply."

A beat of silence passed. Then she faced me, mere inches away. "We both know you aren't a man at all."

I released her like a falconer releases his bird, pushing her off into the waiting embrace of the forest. Veronica hesitated for a fraction of an instant. Her gaze flickered between me and Logan. Then she was gone, her hair a flash among the shadows.

*Goodbye for now, Veronica,* I thought. *For now... but not forever.*

# CHAPTER 9

## VERONICA

*I* spent hours in a barely contained rage after finally making it back to the hotel. The floor creaked under my feet as I paced around the suite in my socks, too worked up to sleep or even shower. Every word that sleaze Orion had said stuck in my brain. I wanted to scrub at my skin until I could no longer feel the unnatural coolness of his fingers on my neck.

"Who the fuck does he think he is?" I demanded out loud. Of course it was a rhetorical question, and unfortunately, his concept of self lined up pretty well with his actual status. As clanmaster in Anchorage, his word was pretty much law, as far as the vamps in his clan were concerned.

The master said to jump, they asked how high. No doubt he had a legion of henchmen at his beck and call. All he had to do was distribute my face to the troops, and I was doomed to have a very bad time.

It had to be a game to him, a muscle he flexed to try and make a fool out of me, and I hated him for it. I hated the way he so obviously viewed me as prey, and the way he had stared as if he was already entitled to the kill. The memory alone made me shudder.

But most of all, I hated my body's reaction to his presence. Orion was not someone who should have held any appeal for me at all, and yet...some hidden magnetism drew me toward his clutches. I thought I'd done pretty well holding my own this last time, but the potential of the future scared me. What if my resolve weakened for an instant?

He'd gotten so damn close. If I closed my eyes, he might as well have been standing right beside me, his presence lingered so strongly. I'd never met a vamp like him, though I had certainly been warned about the old ones, the ones who seemed able to bend the human psyche to their will. Maybe Orion was used to hapless mortal women falling all over him in the blink of an eye.

Then there were his two accomplices. One with black wings, and the other with smoke wafting from the corners of his mouth and nose. Those two weren't vampires, though what exactly they were, I wasn't too sure yet. Demons? Why was Orion with them anyway and not with more of his own kind?

The next couple of days that followed our accidental rendezvous down by the inlet shore were full of me buckling down on my resolve to get to the bottom of the rash of violent crime Lian called me about. The desk in my room disappeared beneath pages of notes I compiled of my findings, complete with drawings, charts, and diagrams. I listed every conceivable reason I could think of as to why a vampire from Seattle might have been found dead so far from home.

Still, despite my best efforts to explore every angle, there were pieces missing. I just didn't know enough about the way the region had developed in the years since I had last been local. I certainly didn't remember such a robust supernatural presence. Then again, I had a lot of other things to think about.

But I did know someone who was more than happy to fill in the blanks. Lian's huge, rambling house began to feel more and more like home again with each visit. We always ended up on the long, overstuffed sofa in the den, covered up by blankets, flames crackling in the fireplace. It was kind of strange to be sitting there all cozy, eating fresh baked goods and drinking from steaming mugs of coffee or hot chocolate while we discussed everything hiding in the city's darkest shadows.

"I'm not sure when it started, exactly." Lian sat cross-legged on the sofa, cradling her mug in her lap. She frowned, thinking. "A year ago, or maybe eighteen months. I was helping Dad with the books, and I started to notice all these new names on the payroll. I mean, like a dozen at a time. So I asked him about it and he told me there was an influx of transplants looking for work."

I raised an eyebrow. "Transplants?"

"That's what he called them. I guess I didn't think too hard about it because it's the kind of thing that happens a lot in Alaska, you know? People get wanderlust and they come up here thinking they can go off the grid or live in the wilderness or whatever. I've heard of whole families relocating here to get a fresh start." She shrugged. "So yeah, it was a ton of people, but it just meant more help for Dad, as far as I was concerned."

"Right." I took a sip of my cocoa and stared into the fire. "And it was probably a huge part of why the boats are doing so well now. Not like he's going to turn down an opportunity to expand if he thinks it's viable."

"Exactly. But one day I was running numbers and I kept having to go back and double check. I thought there must have been a mistake—these guys weren't getting paid nearly enough. And usually that's the kind of thing that will start a riot around here, so I called my dad in a panic and told him we were accidentally shorting some of the fishermen." Her frown deepened slightly. "That was when he told me about the arrangement they made and how he was paying them partially in a percentage of their catch."

"Has he ever done that before?" I already knew the answer, but I wanted to hear it from her.

Lian shook her head vehemently. "God, no. He would've laughed anyone who asked right back out the door. I tried to get him to tell me what was going on at the time. He just said this was a special case, not to worry about it, and to get back to work." She chuckled. "I mean, you know Dad. Work is his life. I just did what he asked."

"Was this around when the violence began?" I leaned over to pour more hot cocoa from a massive thermos on the coffee table. The chocolate-scented steam made me think of the couple of holidays I flew back here after I lost Grandma and spent it in the very same place against the quiet backdrop of snow. Those days had never felt more like a dream.

Lian took a deep breath. I could see her sifting through her memories almost like they were physical objects, grains of sand pouring through her fingers. "I think so," she finally said, although the words were reluctant. "I want to say there had been stories about a crime wave on the news before, but this was when it all started exploding. People in Anchorage were kind of shocked. There are a lot of disappearances up here, but not necessarily outright murder."

"And where were the vamps while this was all happening?" I was slowly working my way toward what was, for me, the real heart of the issue. If Lian or her family had had dealings with Orion in the past, she didn't tell me. Would I have done something if I'd known about him sooner?

"I wish I could tell you." She ran her fingers through her hair. "But I didn't put two and two together for a pretty long time. Not until our guys started going missing. And even then, who's to say it had to be vamps? Alaska's like a three-ring supernatural circus. It could've been anything that was just passing through."

She set her cup on the coffee table, stood up, stretched, and went to poke at the fire. A cloud of sparks kicked up behind the screen.

"Has anyone ever mentioned anyone named Orion?" That was, at long last, the million-dollar question, and it hung in the air for a minute. Lian glanced over her shoulder at me, trying to read my face.

"Orion?" She spoke the clanmaster's name like she was trying out a foreign word. "No, I don't think so." She looked me in the eye. "Who is he?"

"Good freaking question," I muttered. "We ran into each other a couple times. He'd like me to assume he's the one in charge around here." My fingers drummed along the side of the mug. "Pretty sure he's murdered at least two people, so…maybe he's not bluffing."

Lian bristled visibly. "Don't tell me he confessed."

I shook my head, also choosing not to tell her about the humanoid hand I'd seen disappearing below the icy surface of the inlet. "Not in so many words. I think something is brewing in Anchorage."

"Yeah. That's what I've been afraid of." We both fell silent for a little while. The grandfather clock in the foyer chimed the hour of six in the evening.

I was the one to speak up first. "How many employees have you lost?"

"Six." Lian answered so readily I knew she had counted over and over. "Only a couple were ever found, though." Her lips pressed into a grim line. "They were dead, of course."

"And was this before or after you found out they were shifters?"

"Most before," she said. "One of them disappeared after and still hasn't turned up. My guess is that they'll probably be recovered after the snow finally melts."

Her theory resonated with my instinct. Orion had definitely seemed to be taking advantage of the unusually cold, brutal weather. Snow and ice could keep a lot of dirty secrets—for a time.

"Did anything change after you caught them shifting?" The absolute last thing I wanted was for the Zhaos to end up in the middle of whatever messed-up bullshit this turned out to be. I felt a great need to protect them at all costs. If that meant throwing myself straight into the fire of yet another turf war, I'd do it happily.

To my relief, Lian said no. "The guy was surprised," she said with a laugh. "But it was at least as much because he turned back stark naked as anything else." Her nose scrunched. "Those dudes are *hairy*, V. How long is it going to take to forget I've seen that?"

"Too long." I smirked. "Way too long. You don't think they'd consider you a liability or anything, since you're technically a witness?"

"Who am I going to tell?" She arched her eyebrows. "Dad already knows; he has to. The only way he'd pay in fish is if he was paying a literal bear. It's not like they're trying to sneak around behind *his* back. Besides, Alaska's like the land of open secrets. Nobody cares what you are as long as you don't bother them with it."

"That's true, I suppose." The forty-ninth state was nothing if not a haven for outcasts and weirdos of all types. Why shouldn't that rule apply to monsters as well as men? "Still, keep your eyes open, okay? Call me if you hear or see anything suspicious. I will hit the ground running."

"I know you will." Lian smiled. "Because you're the best. And because I'm paying for your room." She hesitated. "You know, you could stay here if you wanted."

"Yeah…no thanks." I sucked in a deep breath, imagining the awkwardness of that conversation. *Lian told me you were hiring bear shifters to work on the fishing boats. Well, they're being murdered by a sexy vampire and two of his friends, so I'm here to sort that out. No big deal.* "It's easier to come and go at night if I'm on my own."

"Good call." Lian looked visibly relieved. She sighed. "I had hoped I might be blowing things out of proportion when I first called you. But the more we talk, and the more questions you ask… That's not really the case, is it?"

I chewed my lip and thought of Orion and his two henchmen standing over the half-frozen corpse they'd pitched into the water. I remembered the vampire's eyes raking over my body, cold, piercing, relentless. His voice echoed in my ears as clearly as if he were standing right beside me.

*I'm not a man to whom consequences normally apply.*

"No," I said quietly. "No, it isn't."

"Think we've talked shop long enough, V. How about I order us take-out and we watch a movie? Dad and Mom are out of town a few days. You can crash here if you want. Will be nice to eat too much food and watch bad movies with you."

Her offer sounded amazing, so how could I knock her back? Especially when she looked at me like she wasn't beyond begging. My mind still churned with everything she'd told me, but I'd also missed spending more time with her where we just had fun.

"Deal." I reclined on the couch, smiling at how good it felt to be at her place. It was rare that I took any time off, my days and nights were usually filled with study and slaying. So this was a nice change of pace.

"Excellent." She started tapping her phone. "There's this new Spanish Tapas place that just opened up and I've been dying to try out their food. I'm going to order a variety of dishes for us."

"I can't wait." Reaching over, I grabbed the remote for the television. "And I'm selecting our movie tonight."

She cut me a serious glare. "Okay, no soppy romances. I want b-grade!"

I scoffed. "I don't do soppy romances."

She fake-laughed, howling loudly. "Says, Ms. I-love-Hallmark movies. You made us watch them each time you returned here for Christmas."

Flicking on the television, I ignored her gloating because clearly Lian never forgot a thing.

# CHAPTER 10

## SETH

The mortal plane was pale compared to hell—pale, desaturated, and painfully boring. I got tired real fast of walking through a miasma of fog every day. Couldn't go a mile without ending up soaked to the skin, freezing rainwater pooling on the ground. I missed the days when flames nipped at my heels, and a trail of smoke heralded my arrival. I was known in my own domain. Hated, maybe. Feared, definitely. But here? Nobody knew who I was.

And I wasn't even allowed to kill anyone yet.

But wandering alone through the damp and dreary night was better than spending hours holed up in the vampire's mausoleum of a house. The more time I spent in his vicinity, the stronger the urge to punch him in his smug, condescending face. Just once, but hard enough that he'd feel it for the rest of his miserable un-life.

Don't get me wrong: it wasn't that I regretted the deal we made where I'd finally gain power over my own realm. To be left the fuck alone so I could do as I wanted without dealing with anyone who pissed me off. To forget my past and start fresh wasn't a big ask, was it?

Contracts had been a way of life for all eternity, and I was used to keeping company I didn't care for. Orion had a singular talent for knowing exactly how to push my buttons—and then doing it all at once. Every day I came within an inch of erupting like some mythical volcano, but I'd gotten very good at reeling back from the edge at the last second. At the end of the day, I understood he offered me a chance to escape my past. He sought me out, asked me to help him, so as much as I wanted to murder him, I remembered the under-lying agreement between us wasn't between two enemies. We just didn't see eye to eye on everything.

For the moment, I made do by roaming the streets, picking over the darkest parts of the city shadows in search of something to hurt, eat, or both. The blood in my veins refused to settle. And dammit, I was hungry all the time.

That night, the usual prowl wasn't enough. I had something else on my mind besides idle violent fantasies of raking Orion across the coals. Every time I closed my eyes, even if it was just to blink, the girl flashed in my mind. The one he'd been tormenting on the night we dropped a body in the river, with her shining eyes and annoyingly bright hair. On the outside, she was so much more than another ordinary plain Jane like the rest of the human women in an endless line of 'em.

I could not stop thinking about her, and I didn't know why. Yeah, she was sexy, yeah I was pissed that Orion had kept her to himself the whole time, but what else was new? The bastard never shared anything important with us. He always had to be the center of attention, as sure as the sun rose every day on this godforsaken place. His ego had never bothered me all that much before.

This time, it drove me insane. Whenever I thought about her skin in the moonlight, or the way she stared at me as I walked by, my body demanded more than a sterile memory. I wanted to know what her body looked like under those winter clothes. How perfect she would be pinned under me in bed, or up against a wall, or just naked on the floor. Anything would do. I wasn't about to be picky.

The burning thoughts nagged at me constantly, a crackling hum in the back of my mind. Never before had I met a human who could sate my lustful appetite, and I had no reason to believe she was up to the task. Yet something about her made me think she might be able to deliver. If only there was a way to test the theory without Orion finding out. No doubt he'd throw a shit fit over someone else playing with his toys.

Which, I had to admit, tempted me more. I could easily get off on the idea of making the vampire mad.

I blew out a thick plume of smoke and told myself to cool it. Shoving my sleeves up to the elbow, I let the misty rain turn to steam as it struck my skin. In the dark of the night, my veins glowed faintly, fiery orange and yellow. There was an itch building that demanded to be scratched, one way or another. Some poor son of a bitch was about to have a very bad evening.

Deep down, I kept wishing it was Orion on the other end of my wrath. He annoyed me more after meeting the pink-haired girl than before. Didn't seem fair that a first-class prick like him coasted along on unlimited time. *Someone ought to number his days,* I thought, and not for the first time. Once, months before, I'd almost done it myself.

A smile crept across my face as I slowed down to savor the recollection. He always kept the doors to the several rooms he called his, locked, as if there was anything in his gaudy, antique junk that anyone would want. But there was one night he'd forgotten, and I heard the door creaking on my way by. Sunrise was just getting underway, and he had pulled the drapes tight over the window.

Hell of a weakness, that sunlight.

The casket was sitting in the middle of the room, sealed tight and surrounded by a sprinkling of what turned out to be dirt. Back then, the notion of Mr. High-and-Mighty vampire having to recreate his own grave to sleep in made me choke back a bark of laughter. Of course he couldn't sleep with a blanket and a pillow. What an asshole.

Well, I hadn't been able to resist the urge to snoop around a little bit. Like I said, most of his things were tasteless, gaudy junk, way too overblown and Gothic for anyone in their right mind. A leather couch sat against the back wall with a small table and lamp. It took about five seconds for all of my attention to focus on the one interesting thing in that room: the casket. Heavy and made out of solid ebony wood, it was polished to a shine, lovingly cared for in a way that gave me, a demon, the creeps.

I remembered reaching out and running my fingers across the lid. How easy would it have been to crack that thing open, dump his stupid living corpse on the floor, and drive the closest stake-like object through his corrupted heart? It was strange to recognize that Orion, and all the rest of his kind, were abominations to me, in a way. Creatures like him were outliers on the fringes of our hierarchy of good and evil. They existed in defiance of death, the strongest and most natural force in the universe.

Maybe that was the real reason he pissed me off. Or maybe I just really wanted to devour the sexy human girl he thought he'd claimed. Either reason worked for me. I did not need to be convinced to despise anything.

The city around me disappeared against the backdrop of my thoughts as I made my way into downtown Anchorage. A cluster of bars remained open, lights weak in the mist. I aimed for them, eyes tracing the sodden pavement. The sound of boots on the sidewalk and my deepening ruminations nearly blocked out all others.

Why hadn't I killed him then? Pragmatism was the answer I liked to give, but cowardice lurked in the realm of uncomfortable truth after he offered me a way out of my problems. The conflict of how I felt toward him drove me crazy.

Somehow, he had convinced me that he was the sole distributor of the prize he had promised—free rein over the mortal realm. He was the one who could loosen my chains and allow me to run amok as I pleased in the land of men. And he ruled over his kind with an iron fist. The other, lesser vampires waited at his beck and call. I could have fought most of them off, but the shadow of a doubt was enough to stay my hand.

At the time, Orion's reasonings, whatever they were, had made sense. And even now, Orion's word was the bond that held me at his side. I was ravenous and restless, but I could also be patient. If he turned out to be a liar, I would simply destroy him. He knew that, too.

But others did not share the same wisdom.

"Hey, freak!"

The taunt snapped me out of my head as quickly as a bone snapped under pressure. I wheeled around in search of its source, reflexive rage rising in my chest. The heat surged from my body; I felt the lowest layer of clothes begin to smolder on my skin.

A low whistle cut through the gloam. "Over here, Smokey."

This time I pinpointed the voice right away. The cluster of vamps leaned up against the walls at the end of an alley, their dead eyes flat in the dusky light. They were not the same maddeningly elegant breed as the bloodsucker I loved to hate. No, these were mongrels, mangy and feral. No scruples at all.

No one would miss them.

They grinned at me as I turned to face them down the narrow passage, mouths stretching to expose hungrily pointed teeth. The ravenousness I could understand, but I wasn't about to give up my own blood.

"Sorry." I rubbed my chin, eyes narrowed. "You talking to me?" All of us were obviously itching for a fight. The air crackled with thinly veiled tension.

"What if we are?" The vamps straightened up, tall and thin and gangly. Two of them cracked their necks and knuckles in anticipation. They thought this was going to be as straightforward a beatdown as they were ever likely to get. A gift from the gods of the street.

But that would make me the sacrificial lamb, and if there was anything I had never been, it was meek and compliant. "Well, then you'd better be ready to have something to show for that bad attitude." Again I pushed up my sleeves. The veins in my forearms burned hot, and I wondered if I should just let the sons of bitches drink my blood. Call it an experiment, see what that would do to them.

The vamp in the lead laughed and spat on the ground. He spoke like his throat had been packed full of gravel. Eyes that should have been bloodshot were spidered with gray capillaries. "You think you're on the high ground, all cozied up with the clanmaster, don't you? Think you're safe in this town?" Their advancing circle began to pull in tighter around me. "Think again."

My least favorite thing about vampires was the inherent difficulty in gauging their strength. Every one of those assholes looked like he had walked straight out of the crypt he'd died in, but experience taught me how easily they could be underestimated. If there was anything I did not want, it was to be shown up by the local stiffs.

"Are we gonna do this, or what?" I sucked in a deep breath, churned it into smoke, and as the first one lunged toward me, blew the whole cloud out in his face. He reeled back and came up choking as I grabbed for his throat through the smoke screen. "Never mind. Guess I answered my own question."

"You cocky son of a bitch!" The vampires leaped on me from either side, clawing at my arms and shoulders with ragged nails like an angry, grotesque flock of birds. I used the one flailing in my grip to shove them off. My hand tightened around his neck. He gagged. His tongue lolled from his mouth. Someone threw a punch into the side of my face, causing stars to briefly explode behind that eye.

I dropped him and swung around to face a different attacker. This one wasn't much more than a scrawny punk, probably a kid struck down and turned out of pity. For all he lacked in muscle mass, he knew how to fight in the way a caged animal fights: with desperate, wild strength. I clenched my fist until it glowed white hot and drove it into the center of his sternum. He howled in pain, and when he staggered back, the imprint of my knuckles was branded on his skin.

The leader of this pathetic little club still

writhed on the concrete, holding his throat. The two who remained knelt at his side. I turned to stare down at them. Blinding heat radiated off my fist. I lifted it and snapped my fingers.

"Want me to burn it all down?" I demanded. "Because I will." All I had to do was apply a little pressure, and he'd be in prolonged agony at the very least.

Then I remembered how I'd have to return to that damn house and face up to Orion about killing some of his men. Didn't matter that they were like plague rats, weak and disgusting. Their beloved clanmaster would have my head. And I couldn't count on Logan for shit.

The realization was a downer, to say the least. Instantly, I felt the adrenaline ebbing, its high spiraling down into an immediate depression. A black cloud formed in my head as I forced myself to step away.

"Where you going?" the vamp croaked from the ground. He pried one hand off his neck and used it to flip me off.

"Hey." I glanced back at him. "A word of advice? Don't press your fucking luck."

VERONICA

I gripped the stake at my belt having just watched Seth battle a handful of vamps. Who started the fight was questionable as I stumbled upon them mere seconds earlier. Though that was enough time to reveal Seth as a man who never backed down and let his rage rule him. Not to mention his ego. Except, he wasn't really a man, was he? With every punch and kick he had delivered, thin threads of dark smoke curled out from the corners of his mouth and nostrils.

I'd seen my fair share of supernaturals, so what was a demon doing out of Hell and in Anchorage of all places?

They were known for their berserker-like fighting tendencies.

Unrelenting.

Ferocious.

Unstoppable.

They were the warriors of the supernatural world and no one volunteered to battle them. Well, unless you were a tribe of idiotic vampires who had no clue.

Fury filled his eyes as he had reached for the throat of another vampire, then dropped him to the ground. It intrigued me that he worked with the clanmaster, yet openly destroyed vamps. Maybe these were Orion's clan enemies? It was hard to tell in all honesty.

Though it was difficult to ignore Seth's strength and power. Something tightened in my chest at seeing how easily he dealt with the vampires, at the way his muscles flexed. One thing was for sure, he was having a blast taking down these fiends.

After a small exchange with the vamp still on the ground, Seth whipped around and walked away from him, his face twisted into a frustrated expression. He was headed right in my direction.

Our gazes locked, and I quickly retreated down the narrow street lined with storefronts. Lowering my hand from the stake, I licked the cold from my lips, and stood tall as he rounded the corner. Of course I expected him to come this way.

"Have you taken to spying just on me now?" he asked, looming over me, wearing all black from his boots to the heavy coat that fell to his waist. The tone in his voice didn't belong to someone angry but carried a playful tone.

"I have better things to do with my time. If you

happen to be in my path, then that's not my problem."

He arched a brow and gave a slight shake of his head as if unsure if he liked my answer. As much as I reminded myself who stood in front of me, my body betrayed me in response to the eye-candy studying me from head to toe.

Never in a million years would I have expected myself to think *that* about a demon, but Seth was unlike any of the beasts I'd encountered. He was built to be a fighter, broad and powerful, yet those solemn eyes and damn perfect lips undid me. The darkness behind his gaze told of heartache, or a broken past. It called to me, drew me to him, and for a short pause, I let myself believe someone like him and me could have something in common. All the hurt and guilt that chewed me up on the inside reflected from his eyes.

"If you keep looking at me that way, I'm going to take that as an invitation, little girl."

My thoughts evaporated, bringing me back to the present and under the watchful eye of a demon.

"That's not happening. Anyway, what was all that about?" I stuck my chin out in the direction he'd just come from. I reminded myself who I dealt with and the danger he posed, the unpredictability. He wasn't a man to let myself lust over.

"Just a small altercation I'm sorting out very soon. So, are we going back to your place or mine?"

I laughed at his presumption. "Keep dreaming. If that's how you come onto women, I bet you strike out a lot."

He drew in a sharp breath and raked a hand through his hair. "I like you. You don't back down. I admire feisty women. And you don't want to know how many women flock to me." That deviously sexy grin split his lips, revealing a white row of perfect teeth.

The air between us thickened, my heart thumping into my ribcage. His yellowing eyes caught the light of the bright sun.

"How about you tell me what you're doing working with Orion?"

"We're business partners," he answered me, smirking through his lie.

Before I knew it, his arm swept around my back, pulling me to him, our bodies pressing together.

My hands snapped up to push against his chest. His rock hard muscles flexed under my touch.

He inhaled the air, then narrowed his gaze on me. "There's something different about you than the other humans, isn't there? But what is it?"

I refused to tell him anything about myself, and I instinctually shoved him, but it was too late to stop losing myself to him or end the feelings he roused deep inside me. He gripped me with enough to strength to know escaping wouldn't be easy, though at the same time, his sheer size and power sent an explosion of butterflies through my stomach.

One touch and I forgot the danger he posed. His hand stroked across my lower back, leaving a streak of fire in its wake.

His face was inches from mine, and I was breathless. I should knee him in the balls and turn away, yet I let myself stay in his arms a bit longer.

"Tell me when to stop," he teased, and his words lit me up from the inside. "I promise to go slow at first."

A flush flared over my body, and as much as I wanted him to do the things he promised in his eyes, it wasn't going to happen.

I drove strength behind my hands and pushed against his chest. "Let me go!"

His hand fell away, and I stumbled from his

grasp. Gasping for air, my whole body tingled with a need I refused to acknowledge.

I clenched my hands by my side. "You can't just go around taking what you want."

"That's where you're wrong."

I shook my head. "Just keep out of my way, okay." I swung away, trembling from how easily he affected me, just as a small gust of warm air rushed across my back.

I glanced over my shoulder and Seth was gone. Yet the earlier arousal still pulsed deep in my core. *What was wrong with me?*

Turning around, I headed down the street and kicked myself for letting Seth get under my skin. He knew exactly what he was doing, and I fell royally for his tricks.

Asshole.

Black coffee was the only mortal indulgence I entertained on a regular basis. Its caffeinated bitterness ran through bloodless veins like a small electric shock, giving everything an edge that was just a little bit sharper. I liked to think it helped me see the world through human eyes.

The brewing and drinking of my coffee had become almost ritualistic in a sense. I had gotten the process down to an art, designed to produce a cup exactly the way I liked it. I was in the middle of pouring the water over a mound of fresh grounds when the front door of the house slammed open. In moments, the pleasantly cutting scent of my coffee was overwhelmed by acrid brimstone.

"We need to talk," Seth snarled from the kitchen doorway. "You and me. Right now."

"Nothing's stopping you." I chose not to turn around. Though it was essential to his very demonic nature and had been from the start, Seth's uncouth manner grated on my nerves more than anything else had in centuries. He knew nothing of respect, nor how to address his superior.

"A pack of your dirty little psychopaths tried to take me out just now." He slammed his fist into the doorframe. The house quaked. "You got anything to say about that?"

"Surely you didn't allow them to think they stood a chance?" He wore the minor marks of a skirmish, not least of which was the purple bruise under his left eye. Its hue contrasted nicely with his reddish skin. "Don't tell me—that one was free, right?"

He stormed across the threshold toward me. "Listen up, Supreme Leader. If you don't get your worthless pack of miscreants under control, I'll call off our arrangement. And then you'd better watch your back."

That was enough to capture all of my attention.

I set the empty kettle on the countertop and met his furious gaze. A matching rage had begun to simmer inside of me, but I held it down. The scaffolding of future plans hung in the balance.

"Are you insinuating that I sent them after you?" I asked calmly. "As if I've forgotten who my allies are? I apologize if they didn't observe proper etiquette toward you. Sometimes the clan's manners come up lacking."

It was his chance to back down and defuse the ticking time bomb sitting between us. But I could see he had worked himself up into a fervor during the walk home, and he refused to be mollified.

"Don't feed me that fancy bullshit," Seth snapped. "Excuse me for thinking a leader ought to be able to control his minions. Let me know if I'm wrong about that."

I bristled. His words were thoughtless, born from a bubbling cauldron of spite, and yet they struck true. I'd already had enough of my authority being questioned in recent weeks. Any more could turn dangerous, especially if the source of dissent was so close. And, as I well knew, letting the demon have his freedom wasn't really an option. I needed to secure his allegiance.

"You're not. But I would caution you to choose

your words carefully from this point forward." Even I was able to hear how drastically my tone had cooled in the past twenty seconds. He had thrown down an unspoken gauntlet, knowing I was not one to back down from such a challenge. The audacity of his boldness failed to endear him to me. We were rapidly approaching a standoff.

"Yeah?" He leaned close to my face. This close, it seemed that the monstrosity of his true nature strained at the seams of his human likeness. "I'd caution you to think about who you really want on your side." He paused to let the words sink in. "Next time, every last one of them will end up dead." A beat of silence passed. He decided to double down. "And I'll take the girl too, just because I know it'll burn your ass."

The world went white. I whipped toward him, lips curling up over fully extended fangs. "You wouldn't dare!" The mere mention of the girl—for I understood exactly which girl he meant—awakened a force of primal jealousy. I had come to think of her as *mine,* and mine alone.

He might disrespect my clan or call my leadership into doubt. But the pink-haired girl? I owned her.

"There it is." He grinned. "I've struck a nerve.

Can't wait until she gets sick of you and starts looking around for something better." The grin widened. "I'll be waiting, I can tell you that much."

"Hold your tongue," I growled. "Or lose it. Your choice."

Now the demon had started to enjoy himself. He took a step back, reveling in my momentary loss of control. "You know, I can't blame you for being scared. You filthy rats are a dime a dozen. I don't think I would've known the difference between your boys and the other ones, come to think of it."

I wished there was someone, anyone, present to appreciate the sheer willpower I exercised in deciding not to screw our agreement and destroy him completely. He was toying with me, an intolerable feeling. I saw myself reaching out and tearing into him so clearly it might have been a vision of the future.

By some miracle of self-discipline, I refrained. The tiny voice whispering that he was still worth more alive than dead prevailed against all odds. My teeth shrank back into my mouth. I managed to put an extra sliver of distance between us. The black tide of destruction slowly ebbed.

"Your ignorance is not my concern," I declared.

He laughed. "Not yet. But I could turn from your solution into your problem real goddamn fast, Orion. Don't forget it."

A lot of Seth's claims could be chalked up to passionate bluster, but this was not an idle threat. His glare held a deadly, solemn seriousness that belied all his melodramatic antics. I knew better than to assume he wouldn't take drastic actions, either to preserve himself or get revenge.

For once, he had managed to trap me in a corner. The fact that the fault lay with my own reckless followers did not escape my notice. I pressed my lips together, focused on a point over his shoulder. My hidden anger spiked and threatened to boil over for an instant, but I quashed it as quickly as possible. He must have sensed the tide of my emotions, however; I saw him smirk out of the corner of my eye.

How dearly I desired to snap his arrogant neck, right where he stood. But sacrifices had to be made in the interest of diplomacy. Taking pains to appear incredibly long-suffering, I let out my breath, ran my fingers through my hair. Behind me on the kitchen counter, the coffee finished percolating. I took the opportunity to swivel away from him.

"Very well," I agreed, somewhat tightly. "I will make sure to speak with the clan about this. Rest assured there will be no more trouble."

"That's right," he agreed. "Even if I need to take matters into my own hands."

He left, and I poured a blistering hot serving of coffee. The side of the mug seared my palm—I clutched it harder, leaning into the pain. My knuckles had gone white. The first sip led me to close my eyes and imagine bounding after him up the stairs, ripping him limb from limb and throwing the pieces out the window onto the lawn below. The ever-coiling spring inside me longed for that sort of macabre catharsis.

But alas, the neighbors wouldn't like displays of dismemberment, would they? And neither would the police. As much as I hated to admit it, I felt the net closing in. There had already been sightings of those West Coast cretins sniffing around the property in search of the one we had so unceremoniously sent off to sea. If only they knew he had probably reached halfway down the Knik Arm by now. Soon, he'd be lost for good.

Unfortunately, as far as the Seattle clan was concerned, the suspicion would only deepen. They were a hundred times more tenacious than the blessedly clueless Anchorage police. To my annoyance, the Seattle vampires were my kin in a very distasteful way. My tricks couldn't fool them forever. After all, not much on the mortal plane could do away with a vampire so effectively that he disappeared into thin air.

Not much, except another of his kind. In that way, I was dreadfully exposed. Who else could it have been?

The coffee was gone in the blink of an eye. I poured another mug and drank it through clenched teeth. The thick, fragrant steam poured into my nose. I let the smell surround me. Then I took my cup and retreated to the sanctuary of my personal chambers. As soon as the door closed at my back, I made sure it was locked. Seth's fury never dissipated right away. And he was not to be trusted in a rage.

The eye of the moon glowed mutely from behind the curtains. I reached over and shut them, closing out every whisp of light. Sitting on the end of the couch in complete darkness, guarding the mug from no one, I allowed myself some minutes of self-pity. How far had I fallen as clanmaster to be held to the whims of a tempestuous, ugly being of fire and lust?

"He is a necessary evil," I murmured aloud, for perhaps the hundredth time since summoning him forth from his cursed realm. "When the work is finished, we will be free of each other, and I'll never be afflicted with the sight of his face again." Usually, that affirmation cleared my mood at least a bit, but not this time. The notion that power had begun to shift, however imperceptibly, clung to the back of my mind. I sat back, placed the cup on the floor, and shut my eyes, letting all thoughts pass away.

The next day came and passed.

Dreams of shadowy figures and indistinct violence crept through my mind, carrying me up into consciousness. I woke with a singular purpose at sunset: to reassert my dominance and draw a line in the sand. This territory belonged to one clan alone. And we would hold it to our deaths.

The moon was rising by the time I stepped out into the quiet house. Logan and Seth were both near; their energies spoke easily to mine. Seth had cooled considerably, to the point where I thought he might almost be cordial. Such a window of opportunity would not last long. I went down to the den and called them like a shaman summoning bonded spirits.

Despite our earlier clash, Seth was the first to appear. He stopped just inside the doorway, regarding me warily. "What's this about?"

"Wait for Logan," I said. "You'll see."

He rolled his eyes, forever the petulant child. "Can you make him move faster?"

"Not any more than you can."

He grumbled, but that was all. A moment later, Logan appeared silently. He glanced between us. "It's all right," Seth stated brusquely. "We decided not to kill each other."

The comment fell on willfully deaf ears. I looked at Logan. "There will be a meeting with the intruders tonight. I'll need you and Seth to cover me."

He nodded. No questions asked. It was a refreshing change of pace.

"Since when?" Seth demanded. "This is the first I've heard about it." He eyed me keenly.

"Maybe you would have known yesterday, had things gone a little differently." Our eyes met. I gave him no ground. Wisely, he chose to pick his battles.

"Fine. Let's go." Without waiting for an answer, he brushed past Logan and stomped out of the house. Logan allowed me to precede him. I had never been able to tell if his cold grace had anything to do with actual respect. He averted his eyes as I passed.

Why did his polite submission feel more like a subtle insult? I wondered if I might catch him laughing behind my back, were I to turn around at just the right moment.

Of course I didn't. I had other, more pressing matters on my mind. Then he and Seth scattered into the night, and I was left to make my way into the heart of the city alone, trusting that their eyes would be watching.

# CHAPTER 12

## VERONICA

It was a good thing I'd gotten so used to being tired. A week into running nonstop, firing on all cylinders to try and get to the bottom of this great Alaskan mystery, I had made the switch from coffee and tea to undiluted energy drinks. My mind and body teetered on the edge of total collapse, but I pushed through the haze of fatigue. There was too much ground to cover.

Even though I had lived here before, it never occurred to me that Anchorage might be an unsleeping city. And yet, every night I stepped out of my hotel room into a different world, one teeming with supernatural oddities. The police reports on television and radio were constantly sprinkled with strange stories of monster sightings, "paranormal activity," sounds of wolves howling at the moon. Most of it ended up being categorized as quintessential Alaskan weirdness, filed away, and only spoken of again in whispers. The city was growing its own mythos right in front of my eyes.

But I knew those reports were more than a bunch of residents with wild imaginations. For some reason, it seemed like the barrier between planes had thinned considerably while I was away pursuing a higher education in Seattle. The more I thought about it, the more it made sense. Alaska's mortal population was already highly transient; why shouldn't vamps and shifters and other reality-defying entities pass through too?

I didn't realize just how many there were. Once I started paying attention to more than the latest vampire drama on the street, I could barely tap into my slayer senses without being inundated by information. The trails of magic and energies overlapped and intertwined to create a constantly changing maze in which a person could get lost if she wasn't careful. It was sometimes hard to separate the chaotic noise of Anchorage's regular paranormal community with the conflict between the vamps.

Still, I did my best to tune everything else out—not that it was always easy. The weave of intrigue hidden in Anchorage's dark side had way too many intricacies to ignore completely. I walked by a dozen shady encounters: people whispering at the back corner tables of clubs and restaurants, huddling under a lamp in the park, slinking around corners to meet up and discuss secret matters. Everywhere I looked was something else to pique my interest.

But focus was everything. Vampires permeated the city like cockroaches in an abandoned building. Blink, and you could miss them, but they were everywhere. It only took a couple stakeouts to start identifying all the major players. As it turned out, Orion's clan was thriving in its numbers—and its backroom dealings. At least, that was what the meetings looked like to an outsider. But then the few times I managed to eavesdrop, I only ever heard them talking in nebulous terms about "negotiations."

My experience with the vamps in Seattle taught me that usually meant some kind of organized crime. And everything about Anchorage—its remoteness, its rustic mystique, its inherent subtext of oddity—lent itself to the development of fertile gangland. I sat in the clubs and bars, my hair tucked carefully away underneath a hat and a hood, and I watched a rotating cast of characters walk in and out of the doors.

Some were great at blending in and only my slayer senses betrayed their true nature. Others, not so much. I saw people shuffling along the walls of the room with skin so pale they almost glowed. One guy had a bald head like a cue ball, its curvature painted with bluish veins. After enough time in the industry, I had learned to spot vamps from miles away. These days, Anchorage was infested with them.

They weren't all locals, either. My first good look at a guy from my own neck of the woods sent an electric shock of surprise down my spine. Of course, I remembered that one of the dead had been a Seattle vamp, but until the moment I saw another, I'd assumed he was an outlier, maybe some vagabond wanderer outcast by his clan. It happened sometimes. Now, however, things looked different. And as the night wore on into the wee hours of the next morning, I counted more and more Pacific Northwestern ghouls roaming the streets.

It was obvious that Seattle's vamp outfit had an away team deployed—to the very place I had been called to, no less. Thinking there was no way these events could be the world's biggest coincidence, I made an extra effort to be unassuming, just in case one of them should recognize me. In Alaska I was a nobody, but my name had begun to make the rounds down south. I knew the vamps in the Emerald City whispered about me.

What the hell were they doing two thousand miles north, trudging into shabby dives out of the slushy, miserable cold? Seattle had plenty of gray days and half-frozen nights; the weather wasn't worth traveling for. Yet, there they were, congregating in scummy droves. Their words, spoken low and often directly into each other's ears, were nothing but a murmur in the distance to me. But every now and then, I got lucky and caught a word or two.

"Clanmaster…disgrace…remove him." This statement was met by a solemn nod of every head bowed around the table.

I studied the surface of my drink, which I'd

been nursing at a snail's pace for the last forty minutes. Were they talking about Orion?

"...missing...dead."

The hair stood up on the back of my neck. They had to be talking about the owner of the hand I'd spotted disappearing into the inlet. Unless it was a brand new, undiscovered body. Leaning forward slightly, I gripped the sides of my glass hard. My fingertips and knuckles went white. If this thread of conversation ended in a viable lead, it would be my lucky day.

But luck wasn't on my side. My focus on the vamp gathering was interrupted by the arrival of a secondary figure striding into the barroom. Tall and brawny, the man looked like he could snap three vampires in half at once. A full beard cloaked his face, and through the open collar of his dirty work shirt, I saw coarse tufts of chest hair exploding outward.

The whiff of salty fish stench following him into the space sealed the deal. The guy was undoubtedly a shifter—and I suspected he worked for Mr. Zhao, at that. His entrance made the air crackle with brand new tension, even as he did nothing except stand there and scan the room. The moment his flinty gaze landed on the table of vamps, he glanced back over his shoulder and whistled, jerking his head.

What followed was a veritable parade of people I could only assume were his brethren. The men came in all shapes and sizes, but they had their aggressive hairiness in common. All moved with the sauntering, self-assured gait of a genuine bear, ignoring the curious glances of other patrons. And they all stank like the daily catch.

I sucked in my breath, shifting in my seat.

My ability to sense danger, inherent in any good slayer, was going off like fireworks in my head. There had been meetings before, but never so well-attended in a place like this. My gut told me something was getting ready to go down.

The first shifter laid a meaty hand on the tabletop between the vamps. He leaned in conspiratorially, as if a man of his size could do anything on the down-low. Nor did he really have any concept of a whisper; where I had strained to hear the vampires talking, his husky voice came across loud and clear.

"Any sign of him?"

The vamp, clearly annoyed by his companion's indiscretion, shook his head and motioned for him to be quiet. Offended, the shifter grunted and turned away. He and his men took up residence at the nearest empty table and proceeded about the business of getting hammered. Some ordered strong spirits, but the vast majority seemed to prefer the economical approach—veritable gallons of shitty beer.

The spectacle of it all would've been funny if it hadn't filled me with such foreboding. I felt my pulse slowly rising as I wracked my brain in an attempt to figure out why they were obviously loitering. Was I about to bear witness to a hit?

And if so, could I stop it in time?

The seconds began to crawl. Each minute felt like an hour there in that stuffy, poorly lit hovel. I'd forgotten all about anyone who wasn't at those two tables.

At least until the door opened again. By now, the place was starting to get a little packed, and for a moment, I couldn't get a good look at whoever had just come in. Then a wave of energy smacked me in the face. More vamps, but not from Seattle.

The natives were in the house. Their presence appeared to change the game; all the players knew it. Every head at the tables locked within my sight turned toward the front of the bar. The shifters stopped their half-drunken carousing. The air in the bar grew thick with something other than cigarette smoke and booze.

One of the vamps from Seattle spoke first, sneering at the newcomers. "What do you want? Come to cry about being forced off your own turf?" He laughed mockingly. "Save it, you hillbilly assholes. We've got other things to worry about. Like, say, what we're going to do with all your land once we finish smoking you out."

"Big words from a shrimpy little man," the Alaskan growled. He was, in fact, not so much taller on his own, but his words lit a match in a room full of gasoline. "Why don't you back 'em up with some power?" For emphasis, he beat a fist against his chest. His cohorts drew up around him like a starving pack of wolves. I could see the bare bloodlust in their eyes. "Oh, right. You don't have any here."

Instantly, everyone was on their feet. Several chairs toppled over, and the sound of a heavy glass mug shattering cut through the noise. Around me, the bar's other denizens also stood up, some heading for the exit, some vying for a better vantage point to see the action. My view had been blocked by a few of the burliest shifters, but the rapidly raising voices left little to the imagination.

My pulse spiked, the tension close to bursting.

"Come on, dickhead!" shouted someone with a shrill, nasal tone. "I'll make a goddamn rug out of you!"

I rolled my eyes. Then a primal roar ripped through the air. Behind me, a woman screamed. I saw the dark, rugged form of a gigantic grizzly loom up on two legs in the middle of the crowd, claws out, fangs glistening. It smashed one of the downed chairs with one great paw, sending the wooden frame soaring. I had just enough time to duck out of the way before it crashed into my table and sent splinters everywhere.

"You think you're tough?" the Alaskans jeered. "You ain't shit! Who's getting their asses run out now?"

It only took a few seconds for the barroom to dissolve into utter chaos. Soon, chairs weren't the only things flying around. I dodged a table, a heavy serving tray, and a barrage of glasses. My heart pounded in the chest at being caught in here, but I made no effort to leave. If a fight was going down, then why not take the chance to eliminate some of the foe.

The floor sparkled with shards of broken cups. My footsteps crunched as I crouch-ran for cover.

All of a sudden, I found myself in the middle of a warzone, and a shiver raced down my spine.

Still, I couldn't resist the urge to sneak a look. A frenzy of sounds threatened to overwhelm my senses. As I peered over the top of an overturned booth, the scene in front of me didn't make much more sense. Shifters and vamps clashed together in one horrific, writhing mass, slashing, biting, striking at each other. At least one vamp lay sprawled on the floor, stunned. The bears had already shed a ton of blood.

Telling anyone apart had become impossible. All of the energy churned together into a dizzying miasma of signatures. I couldn't have said who was coming out on top if my life depended on it. Nor was I aware that the bar had emptied of its previous crowd. Survival instinct had driven every single person into the streets.

Everyone but me.

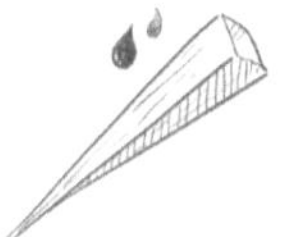

There's not much I hate more than showing up late to a good party. That's how you miss all the fun. And that was almost what happened when we got to the heart of the city. I was itching for some real action, something more fun and visceral than carting around a guy who was already dead. I wanted to be part of the process this time. To be there when it mattered.

And I was the one who smelled the fight first. It was the animal halfbloods that led me there; they reeked for miles. That, and the scent of spilled blood. Once I got a whiff, I was on it like a hound. For once, Orion and I had ended up on the same page. We tracked the trail all the way to the door of that hole in the wall. Stepping across that beat-up threshold was like stepping into my own personal paradise.

But like I said, we were late, and the battle-ground was messy. Looked like some vamps had taken a serious, no-joke beating. In fact, it looked like most of them were still in the process of getting their asses whooped. The shadows seethed with the huge, menacing silhouettes of the bear-hybrids, glaring from the dark like rabid monsters.

"Come on," I muttered to Orion. We were side by side at the front of the room, staring down this catastrophe of a scene. "Let me put 'em down. It'll only take a second." I wasn't exaggerating. The hybrids were all bark and no bite. Not much more than teddies, as far as I was concerned.

But Orion held up his hand. "Wait."

I could've strangled him and staked his heart with one of the chair legs scattered on the floor, and I'd have been lying if I said the thought didn't occur to me. Every nerve and muscle in my body was alive and twitching. I was born for this kind of carnage, and yet he had the audacity to deny me? A blazing hunger for violence gnawed at the pit of my stomach. How could he expect me to stand idly by?

Near the back of the room, a bear and a vampire hadn't quit duking it out. I watched the bear-man tear a gash the width of the vamp's whole chest, with barely any payoff. Not much blood either, meaning this vamp was starved so he didn't bleed as much as he should from such a deep cut. The flesh hung ragged—but goreless—from its frame. Still, the vamp screeched in pain, a sound like music to my ears. He bolted away from the bear, vaulting haphazardly over a minefield of ruined furniture. As he disappeared behind an overturned booth in the opposite corner, I caught a flash of movement and a short, involuntary shriek.

As if attuned to that specific noise, Orion's head snapped around. He stared hard at the booth, and I realized he had been searching for something all along. We were both watching as the wounded vamp popped back up and tossed something—someone—out into the open. The girl kept her balance just barely, the floor squealing under her feet.

She straightened up, and a lock of bright pink hair tumbled out from under her hat. Orion's gaze sharpened.

"God damn it," I mumbled. Whatever our original mission had been, I knew enough to consider it derailed once he'd positively identified her. The bitch was priority one in his mind, judging by the way he eyed her up like he could see every inch of her skin. But he had to act fast, because he wasn't the only interested party. The bears and the remaining vamps had all congregated around her.

Everything in the place wanted a piece of her ass. And if she didn't do something about it quick, there was going to be trouble. The circle had already begun to close in around her.

"Never mind," Orion said abruptly. His voice was frigid and hard. "Go get her."

I had never been so happy to do anything he said. A surge of searing heat leapt from my body as I charged through the barricade of vamps and shifters. The sudden hot glow from my skin sent the vamps scurrying backwards, hissing, teeth bared. From the sheath on my belt, I pulled out my knife, brandishing it with a flourish.

"Get close. I dare you." The challenge was real and made in earnest. There was nothing I wanted more than to obliterate all of them in as delightfully cruel a manner as possible. Thankfully, a vampire obliged me. He was scrawny, all sinew and bones, his eyes bulging out of his face. Starving, probably so not much blood in his system. The madness of bloodlust was written all over him.

He didn't see the knife coming, didn't even try to turn away. It felt like cheating, the way the blade sank between his ribs with almost no resistance. I yanked it out and watched him drop, wheezing through a lung that was now most likely punctured. Goggle-eyed, he stared straight ahead like a fish that had been dragged from the water.

I turned back briefly to Orion. "Don't you guys regenerate?"

He was shielding his eyes and facing away from me. "Not in the light. Hurry up."

"Oh." I looked down at the glow from my skin, which was rapidly approaching white hot. "Right. My bad." To the rest of the vamps, I said, "Who's next?"

Some of them scattered, the cowardly rats. A few of the braver vermin leapt toward me. It was fun to watch them try to protect themselves from the scorch of hellfire even as they reached to tear at my face and arms. Long, unkempt nails raked over my skin. I reveled in their screams of pain. The scent of roasting meat filled the air, although vamp flesh always smelled a little rotten. I would have happily stayed there until they'd all burnt to piles of char, but alas, the bear-hybrids were on the move, and so was Orion's little girlfriend.

She disappeared from my sight as the vamps got up their courage and piled on. It felt like a dozen clammy hands grasping, scratching, gouging at all the places they might hurt me the most. Sheer terror, for a mortal. For me, the sensation was closer to nostalgia. A sea of desperate, ravenous hands reminded me of a place where I was revered and free to do whatever the hell I wanted—like tear those hands clean off.

The vampires did not react well to being relieved of their appendages. Harsh shrieks of pain and outrage colored the air that only intensified as I started to fling the assailants off of me, one by one. They hit the floor scrambling for purchase. The first one I staked hadn't quite regained his feet. He fell back instantly into a flaccid heap. The snarl on his lips melted down into a blank stare. I lunged forward, loving every moment.

## VERONICA

The back of a meaty hand clipped the side of my head, so suddenly, so fast, I saw stars as I was sent crashing into a wall.

In a flash, I pushed back into the chaos in the bar, my heart pumping furiously, my gaze settling on the bear shifter in my way. He might not have transformed yet, but the smirking asshole was as big as one in human form.

"Don't waste your time, girl," he snarled, his gaze leering over my body. "Only one thing you're good for, and it ain't fighting." He reached down and groped his dick over his jeans, and I gagged.

Fury burned through my veins. I licked the blood from the corner of my lip, closing the distance between me and the brute. He didn't budge but took his eyes off me and focused on the battle around us. That was a mistake.

I threw a roundhouse kick, my heel slamming into his chest. The idiot stumbled backward, but chortled like a pig. Little did he know, my intention wasn't to make him fall... not right away. But rather nudge his huge mass.

The back of his knees suddenly bashed into a

fallen chair, and his eyes widened as he tumbled backward, arms flailing outward for purchase.

All that went through my mind were Lian's words about the dead girls found in town since the arrival of the bear shifters.

Not wasting a second, I leaped toward him, fingers gripping the hilt of my blade.

The chair snapped under him, breaking and he hit the ground hard.

Crash landing on his chest, I shoved my knee into the curve of his throat, my blade pointed at his eye.

"Just imagine if I was a decent fighter, asshole."

His fist came flying for my head. In haste, I slashed my knife outward, the blade biting across his forearm. Blood bubbled instantly.

He roared, bucking his hips, his other arm latching onto me around the neck.

I cracked the end of the hilt right into the side of his head, so hard, I was certain I heard a snap.

Eyes rolling upward, he collapsed onto his back, the tension from his body melting beneath me.

Suddenly, someone grabbed my hair and wrenched me backward. I cried out from the sharp pain zigzagging across my skull, while I flung my blade over my shoulder. The knife sang threw the air, not hitting the mark.

Moments later, the grasp on my hair disappeared, and I fell. Rushing to get up, I whipped around, weapon raised. I came face to face with Orion. He was driving a fist into a bear shifter's gut. So powerful, his attack sent the assailant soaring into a group of vamps.

As they fell, Seth, who'd been in the middle of the vampire circle, came into view. He punched two of the scum at once, pivoted around and kicked another aside, sending him across the room. His strength was phenomenal, and a tingle zipped up my spine at watching the way he fought with such brutal ease. There was definitely something captivating to watch a powerful man like him and Orion fight. I suspected Logan would be similar, if he were in our company.

The whole time Seth smiled like he was on a rollercoaster having the time of his life. The pits of hell burned in his eyes, and the fight was where he came alive. I started to understand why Orion kept him so close. Seth was the muscle for the clanmaster, though I still didn't understand why a demon would partner with a master vampire.

"You're welcome," Orion's voice drew my attention to him as he looked my way with a grin. "Now, get out of here."

I cocked an eyebrow. "Firstly, I was fine without you, and secondly, fuck off."

He tsked and reached over so fast, I had no chance to react. He gripped me by the side of my head as his thumb wiped the blood from my lower lip. "While I love you talking so filthy, now is not the time for dirty talk. I don't want you hurt."

I shoved his hand off me. "I don't need to be wrapped in cotton." Everything about him infuriated me, drove me insane, and more than anything, I hated myself for still finding him attractive. Yet, even as he stood tall before me, blood splashed on his cheek and the blue of his shirt, that tempting tingle curled in the pit of my gut. Strong cheekbones, a captivating gaze against waves of thick hair, and the body of sinner, he was everything I shouldn't have wanted yet craved insatiably.

I swung away from him as two huge men stepped forward, one of them partially transformed, his arms furry and clawed. A shiver gripped my spine. One swipe and he'd tear my head off.

I tensed, tightening my hold on my knife, legs slightly bent as I readied to dive out of the way.

Sneering, the big guy with bear arms unleashed a roar, spittle flying in every direction from his mouth. His buddy heaved each breath, his chest rising and falling faster.

A shadow fell in alongside me, and Orion's arm pressed against mine. "I take the furball. You can handle the smaller one, right?"

I cut him a glare. "You can be such a prick."

"I don't want you harmed and you think I'm the bad guy here?"

The bears came at us, and I pivoted in their direction. In haste, I hurled my weapon at the furry one, hitting him dead square in the center of his chest.

He staggered, growling, pawing at the knife in his chest frantically.

"You're welcome." I tossed the words at Orion as he studied me with a look I couldn't decipher. A cross between anger and admiration. I doubted the clanmaster understood the meaning of that word, but I still smirked at him.

I charged toward the so-called smaller man. Except, there was nothing freaking small about him.

My hand fell to my belt, and I grabbed the staff. One flick and it extended two feet. I ducked from the monstrous punch flying my way. While low, I grasped the weapon with two hands and bashed it madly at the side of his shins. Enough force smacked into him that he collided into his friend being punched to hell and back by Orion.

Swinging back up, I whacked the staff against the brute's back, then another to the side of his face.

Fury burned across his cheeks, and my skin pricked with the energy of his transformation.

Shit! I didn't want him in animal form... these bears were stronger, more resilient that way.

I flicked my staff to retract and collected the stake from my belt instead. The sharp end would do enough damage while I was short a knife.

In that same second I pushed forward to finish this, Orion veered in our direction and thrust himself at the transforming bear. The explosion of growls, arms and legs boomed, and I sighed that he stole that from me.

The sounds of war encased me, vampire against vampire against bear. Goddamnit, how many of them were there.

Orion climbed to his feet, the two bears at his feet, bleeding all over the place. "Now where were we," he said, eyes locked on me, smiling deliciously.

"You were leaving me the hell alone," I answered, despite the fire he ignited in me when he stared at me that way.

In two long strides, he reached my side and scooped an arm around my waist, dragging me against his side. The movement took me by surprise, and my stake slipped out of my hand, cluttering to the floorboards.

Fury surged through me, and I bucked against him. "Get off me, or I'll drive my stake so deep in your heart, it'll—"

"Not happening." He kicked my weapon into the tangle of legs where others fought.

The reality was painfully embarrassing to say the least, that he treated me like a doll.

I drove my fist into his side, but he didn't so much as flinch, his grip squeezing me to his side, his fingers like iron digging into my ribcage.

"You know you're pissing me off even more by pulling this caveman shit!"

"I adore you too sweetheart, but this is our battle, not yours. Now, where the fuck is Seth?"


## SETH

pulled out a chair leg from one nearby and spun around with it outstretched. The vamps who'd advanced upon me drew back, hissing. The fire oozing from my palm ate lazily away at the dry wood. A thin reed of smoke curled up from my grip.

I grinned. "Didn't like that, did you?" If the angry silence was any indication, I had the vamps all out of action. Furious eyes flicked from the blunt end of the stake to my face, as if weighing the pros and cons of another direct attack.

"Intruder!" The biggest vampire snatched for the stake.

I jerked it away and jabbed it at him, playfully.

He glowered. "Infidel! How dare you trespass on our ground!"

"Well, from the sounds of it," I replied, "I'm not the only trespasser here, am I?"

"Seth." Orion laid his hand on my shoulder, subtly easing me backward.

I looked at him at the same time that I shrugged his hand away. "What?" The first time I'd gotten the opportunity to have a little fun, and he was already ruining it. Then I noticed he had the girl with the pink hair tucked under his arm. She was clearly pissed about the arrangement. I snorted.

Orion pushed her firmly at me. "Take her out of here. I'll deal with these cretins." Over his shoulder, I spotted what appeared to be the dead carcasses of several bear-hybrids in an ever-expanding pool of blood. Evidently, the boss had put on a horror show while I was busy.

But now I resented being yanked out of the midst of a good time. He was the one who liked her so much, so why couldn't he escort her himself? Better yet, she could simply be killed on the spot or left at the mercy of the enemy.

"Are you serious?" My temper got the best of me before anything else. "I'm the best fighter you've got and you're going to sideline me to be her bodyguard?"

"Hey!" Mortal danger hadn't dampened the girl's natural spice. She glared at me. "I'm perfectly capable of holding my own, thank you very much. Now release me." She swung her gaze up to Orion then at me. That was when I saw she too was splattered in blood. A streak of it crested her cheekbone like a stripe of rusty warpaint.

I had to admit, blood looked good on her. Next thing I knew, dual desires fought for dominance within me. The stubborn, authority-despising part of me wanted Orion to fuck off forever and let me do my thing in peace. But I also knew I could make good use of a little time alone with this girl. And that made playing the role of a dutiful lackey seem not so bad.

"Do as I say," Orion warned. "Or else." The guy could be so damn dramatic.

I shrugged. "If you're sure, fine. I just figured you might want to take care of her yourself." I wasn't wrong about that—his disdain for handing her over to me was plain as day. In that light, I was happy to take possession of her. The muscles in her arm tensed as we made the transfer. Coiling for a punch, maybe? "Settle down, sweetheart," I told her. "No amount of piss and vinegar is going to get you anywhere at this point."

"Fuck you!" The expression on her face was completely impassive, betraying nothing. When I walked, she walked, but it wasn't the restrained gait of a prisoner. She kept her head held high, chin up, eyes defiant.

That attitude made me want her so bad. And I could sense Orion's eyes on us while we moved farther and farther out of his reach. It was killing the smug bastard to see his prize entrusted to someone else. I knew he wanted to chase after me and threaten to wring my neck until my head spun all the way around if I so much as glanced at her the wrong way. But he had other concerns, such as the small herd of vamps and a few bears still occupying the bar. To them, Orion was no one's friend. He had no choice but to let us go.

I rode the high of that satisfaction for minutes, leading the girl in the same way a farmer leads a stubborn mule.

"You can let me go, now," she snapped, tugging from my grip, but I held her tighter. She remained rigid and unyielding the whole way away from the bar. I admired her strength.

"Tell me how you ended up in the middle of that brawl, or were you following me again?" I asked, after a long pause of silence. "That was no place for a mortal."

The girl frowned. She flicked her pink forelock back from her face. "Who said I was just a mortal?" Her gaze stayed fixed directly ahead, but I wanted her to look at me when we spoke. I remembered she had jewels for eyes.

"Maybe I jumped to conclusions." I doubted,

but I played her game. I reached under her chin and turned her face toward me, just hard enough that she wasn't able to resist. It was not my intention to hurt or destroy her. The more time I spent in her uniquely otherworldly presence, the more I came to understand that she was a trophy of some real value, to be handled with care. Why, I couldn't quite say.

"I'd say so, yeah." She tugged against my hold, and her resistance showed no signs of lessening, which only increase my desire exponentially. "Look, do us both a favor and don't try to connect with me, okay? It's not going to work."

"At all?" I tugged her a little closer, into the sphere of heat from my body. Her breath caught slightly in her throat, which made me smile. I loved having that kind of effect on her. "How about if the connection is purely physical?" My hand slid down her arm until I reached the bare skin of her wrist. She shuddered slightly as we touched skin to skin for the first time. It was then that I gave her a little taste of warmth. A preview.

She tried not to react, but I saw the way her eyes widened for a fraction of a second. She might not have admitted it, but the girl was hooked. As I moved in to kiss her soft, full lips, I thought about how infuriated Orion was going to be. I thought about how he might actually try to kill me.

And then I put my mouth on hers. Consequences could come later. It was time for pleasure.

# CHAPTER 14

## VERONICA

Seth tasted like sharp, acrid smoke that left a sweet burn on my tongue. I didn't want to want him. The moment the shock of his boldness had left my system, I shoved him back, breaking us apart. Still, he lingered for longer than I liked, and his eyes held mine unfalteringly.

I wished he was hideous, like I had grown up believing all demons were. If only this hellish creature's vicious, brutal reality were reflected in his face. But no; he was cruelly handsome, his sharp features somehow only enhanced by his simmering rage. Short dark hair sat messed up from the breeze, eyes that never left me seemed to slide right through my soul. Behind them, I was certain I saw a flame that most likely connected him with the pit of Hell where he came from.

"Excuse me," I protested, a little too breathlessly. "I barely know your name."

The demon smirked. "But you *do* know it." The tip of his index finger curled under my chin, propping my face up so I couldn't avert my eyes. "Say it. Out loud."

His demand felt like sacrilege, but I wasn't able to articulate why. My brain, which I tried to keep so calm and collected under these exact circumstances, had been totally turned on its end, all the thoughts inside churning and flustered. Did I even remember my *own* name?

I clamped my lips shut tight and shook my head. He threw his head back and laughed. The sheer power in his joy chilled my bones. There was a distinct, yet unspoken acknowledgement that everything he did or said was at my expense, an express intent to exploit me for his own gain. I shouldn't have been into it. Not even a little bit. But I was. Each time I'd crossed paths with him, that intensity and curiosity inside me heightened even more. Whatever was going on between us, I craved to let myself fall, to see what it would be like to have such a dangerously gorgeous demon show me a different kind of attention.

When he kissed me again, so fiercely I felt his heat radiate through my whole body, I failed to stop him.

Looking back on the moment later, I had no excuse. Maybe I would've tried to justify my consent by pointing out that I hadn't gotten laid in months, that schoolwork and vamp slaying left no time for any kind of relationship, including a one-night stand, and my body was starved for physical attention. I might have admitted that despite being the embodiment of true evil—or perhaps because of it—he knew exactly what to do with his tongue.

By the time he'd made his way to my neck and shoulder, I was weak at the knees, stifling a moan. The way he touched me made me want to fall to the floor in his arms. My fight or flight senses tingled through every rough kiss and demanding caress. His hands began to roam over every inch of skin he could uncover.

"C'mon," he murmured. His lips brushed the skin just below my right ear. "Say my name." One hand snaked around my waist and planted its palm firmly on my ass. He squeezed. "Take any longer and I won't ask so nicely."

I huffed and glared at him, determined to give up no hint of satisfaction. "What, Seth? That what you want?"

He narrowed his eyes. "I'll give you credit for your guts and your tits."

Another kiss stole my breath. My fingers clenched around the front of his shirt. I was starting to get used to the near-bitter way he tasted; frankly, I was starting to enjoy it somewhat. And I knew he had the ability to work out what my body didn't want him to know.

"Why don't we make the most of our little unsupervised visit?" he suggested. His bright, keen eyes leered at me, and for a moment, the unabashed eeriness of his gaze was enough to snap me out of my trance of desire. Smart, rational, no-screwing-demons Veronica prevailed.

"One, no." I shoved him backward hard enough to catch him by surprise. He came within a hair's breadth of losing his balance and sprawling back-ward onto the ground. "Two, fuck off. We are *not* doing this today. For any reason."

Seth recovered himself quickly. He straight-ened his clothes, ran a hand through his hair, and stared at me with a coldness in his expression that cut like a knife. I knew by his face that running would be useless. He'd catch me, and after that, who knew what would happen? Would he tear me limb from limb and devour my organs? Would he chain me to a radiator and force me to fulfill his every command? My battles usually consisted of facing off vampires, sometimes shifters. But demons...that was a first.

All I understood for sure was that nothing could be put past him. He was ruthless, and he'd made it clear that I had something he wanted.

My only option left was to fight. To that end, before he had the chance to move another muscle, I put my head down and rushed him. On the face of it, the effort was pretty futile. He stood at least a foot taller than me, built like a brick wall forged in hellfire. My shoulder drove no higher than the base of his sternum. I didn't have to check to know the impact was almost nonexistent.

"Seriously?" He caught me by the shoulders in a bruising grip. "Cut it out." The irritated, condescending tone of his words pushed my blood to the boiling point.

"All you have to do is let me go." I had not gone through a year of grueling slayer training to be patronized by an example of the very abomination I was taught to take down. That was why I hauled off and punched him in the face. His head snapped back. I saw his eyes roll. But then he countered so fast there wasn't time to see it. Next thing I knew, his hands had locked around my wrists and pulled them together above my head.

The jolt of pain through my shoulders hurt so much my eyes teared up. I refused to let those tears spill over. If I had anything to say about it, he would never know he hurt me.

"I admire your idiocy," Seth admitted. He licked his lips as he looked at my body. "And now you're going to pay for acting up. You're lucky I believe in rewarding acts of bravery."

Immediately, he tossed me over his shoulder and strode off. His arm locked around my legs, ensuring I wasn't going anywhere.

Anger bubbled in my chest, and I thrashed against him. "You prick. Put me down."

"Keep sweet talking me."

No one was around to spot us, and not that I'd drag any innocents into facing a demon. I had to watch the lights of downtown recede farther and farther into the distance. What replaced them was an endless army of trees and the foreboding voice of the river.

*Okay, V,* I thought. *How long can you hold your*

*breath? Oh yeah, and survive in water that's full of ice?* A few times, I struggled, but the demon simply held me tighter. He spanked me, hard, and ordered me to "Behave."

I flinched that he did that. I thanked everything holy that he couldn't see me biting my lip. Why did it feel so deliciously enticing to let him manhandle me? Why wasn't I just mad as hell about it, instead of mad and vaguely intrigued?

Seth carried me into a house, up some stairs, and into a bedroom on the second floor. I studied everything and the path he brought me through the house for an easy escape. There, he unloaded me onto the bed. In the same swift motion, he pulled the hat off my head. My hair went flying everywhere, bouncing off the mattress. He tossed it aside.

"So what happens now?" I made sure to be extra snarky-sounding, lest he get any ideas about what I thought of him. It wasn't that my overall opinion was changing—a demon from hell with a six-pack was still a demon from hell. I just happened to be turned on by his particular brand of bad attitude. Did I regret that? Yes. Was it preventing me from teetering on the edge of some truly awful decisions? Nope.

I pushed to get up, but he kneeled next to me, claiming my mouth once more. My lips stung from where the bear shifter had punched me. Though, I easily forgot that as Seth kissed me with hunger, with a desperation like he might lose me, which was surprising. I should have shoved my hands into his chest, but my body had other ideas. There was no denying the attraction I felt for him.

Following my desire over my logic, I cupped his face, returning the passion, giving into my whims. My head screamed to get the hell out of there, but my body and excitement took charge. That moment when I craved someone so intensely, nothing else made sense. I cursed him for being so sexy, and well, I was a big girl and knew exactly what I was getting myself into. Even if it was with the enemy. A one-night stand with a hunk I'd regret later, but in that moment, I wanted what he offered. Call me crazy, but I craved more. Life ended too fast, and I promised myself to never hold back on what I wanted. Plus, at the back of my mind, I kept thinking that getting closer to a demon came with benefits, like getting him on my side, gaining insider information, and playing with his thoughts. He might be turning me on, but I intended to have the exact same impact on him…ongoing.

He broke our kiss and reached down beside the bed, then came back up with a length of hefty rope in his hands, which he snapped like a belt. My heart skipped a beat. "Don't take this personally," he said, tying my wrists to the top two bedposts. "Call it insurance for when I'm at my most distracted, and you sweetheart are unpredictable."

"You have no idea," I answered.

The pull of the rope was just shy of uncomfortable. If I shifted too much, I could feel the rasp of the cord on my exposed skin. In a strange way, I enjoyed hearing he tied me up because he feared me.

With my legs free, I clenched my knees tightly together, but he pulled them apart with ease. I saw how easily my body betrayed me. I did find it interesting that he didn't tie up my ankles, giving me the option to still hurt him. Guess he liked to play with danger as much as me.

But when Seth traced his fingers up the inside of my thigh, I forgot everything.

A moan rolled over my throat as heat flared through me, collecting specifically over the apex between my legs.

He examined my face for a reaction, and I swear I did my best not to let him see one. But my cheeks burned, no matter what. He liked that by the look of his grin.

"More of a devil than an angel, aren't you?" he murmured.

"I'm going to kill you for teasing me." I craned my neck to stare him dead in the eye. "Maybe not today or tomorrow, but someday you'll pay tenfold."

He leaned down over me, our lips once again mere inches apart. "I look forward to it, slayer."

Of course he had worked it out. Whatever my preconceptions might have been about evil demon sex, Seth defied most of them. He was not a romantic, tender lover, but he was full of passion and power. I found an undeniable thrill in the way he had so effortlessly rendered me at his mercy. Unbuttoning my thick jacket, he drove the fabric of my shirt up. I gasped as his hungry, hot mouth roamed across the pale plain of my chest and stomach. Tugging down on the fabric of my lace bra, he lingered with rapt attention on each nipple.

I couldn't help but squirm, my desire melting my panties. Licking my lips, I moaned, eager to not feel anything but blissful pleasure.

How could a demon's tongue be so dexterous? My hands, suspended by the rope, clenched automatically. And it was incredible to feel this way. He undid the waistband of my jeans and pulled them down. To my annoyance, my panties were visibly still on me.

Seth smiled wickedly. He pulled the crotch of the underwear aside and teased me with one long finger. My hips rocked up to meet his attentiveness. The feel of his touch had every inch of my body igniting. My heart raced, my nipples hardened. I had no intention to stop when he promised me so much more.

"Hell, I fucking hate you," I breathed, already writhing for more.

"Yeah?" The smile stretched into a cocky grin. "Prove it." Without waiting for an answer, he kissed and licked a sensual trail down to my pelvis. I half expected him to torment me with interminable teasing, but there was no pause before he was ravenously devouring me. Stunned by the sudden shock of pleasure, I gasped. He responded by gripping my ass with both hands and delving deeper into my folds. I shoved my hips into him.

"Oh my God. I want to kill you..." The threat came out in a moan of ecstasy. Every muscle in my legs and abdomen tightened as I strained to get the most out of what he was doing to me. His tongue danced around my clit, and then he sucked it greedily, growling into me. The sound I made wasn't quite human. *"Fuck!"*

A river of arousal flooded through me, the pressure building and building, the sensation of his tongue unbearably insane. But if I thought his mouth was relentless, I had no idea what was in store. He pulled me to the edge of a wild orgasm, only to back off at the last second. I was writhing and trembling in my restraints, dripping wet, covered in sweat. He traced the outer edge of my entrance. I squirmed some more.

"Beg for it," he ordered.

I would rather have died on the spot. "Fuck you," I managed between heavy breaths. "Shut up and fuck me."

Annoyed, Seth leaned back between my legs, his lips on my inner thigh, and suddenly, sharp teeth bit into my skin. Not hard enough to tear skin, but enough to leave a bruise.

"Hey!" I bucked to throw him off, even if his form of punishing me only intensified my already building arousal. He had not appreciated my flippant reply, and I felt his displeasure in the way he climbed over me, his hand wrapped nonchalantly around my neck. Pleasure, pain, and panic surged through me, as they each vied for dominance over my body.

Unbearable desire seemed to win out as I leaned back, eager for this, unable to stop myself if I tried. That was the problem, wasn't it? I should have stopped myself and him but I craved this as much as him. An upspoken lure pulled me to him, and all I could think was, fuck it! Was it so wrong to follow my instincts, my lust for a change?

He pushed into me slowly at first, then filled me up and rode me hard. The bedposts creaked and swayed as if they'd come crashing down on me at any second.

His hands rapidly went from hot to burning. He released my throat and groped my breast. Every thrust brought a new, pounding wave of incredible pleasure, the kind I knew would leave me sore in a few hours. It was so wrong in all ways, but still so amazing. We climbed toward a dizzying peak, my body arching, my pelvis rocking to meet his every thrust, and then he started to back off, to deny me that climax.

His strokes alternated between roughly wild and long and slow, a pattern that kept me on the very edge for an agonizing amount of time. I threw my head back in frustration. If this was a game, two could play. Whatever rise he was trying to get from me stayed firmly under wraps. My torture became his as well as his lips tightened, his chest rising and falling faster, waiting for me to back down first to beg for it.

The demon held out for as long as his innate indulgence would allow. Eventually, as I knew he would, he finally snapped and mounted me with renewed vigor. The sensation of being fucked so hard and deeply filled all my senses to bursting. I gripped the rope and let out a carnal, orgasmic scream. Seth's answer was to reach down and rub directly on my clit.

And I came so hard I saw stars. The force of it left rope burn on both contact points as my body spasmed and bucked underneath him. One of the ties snapped in the throes of my pleasure. I almost punched him again. I clenched his cock inside me, causing him to hiss with undeniable pleasure.

Still deep inside me, Seth roared his satisfaction, pulsing within me. He was like an earthquake —one big tremor followed by waves of aftershocks. It wasn't clear how long we lay in the mess we had made of the bed, dazed. At some point, he roused himself long enough to cut my other arm down as I clung to him, my hands grasping strong, round shoulders.

I collapsed on the rumpled bedspread.

"That's what you get for talking back," he told me casually.

"Well, joke's on you." I sat up, breathing heavily, swooning in the most incredible sex, and made an attempt to fix my disheveled hair. "Because now I kinda want to do it even more." There was no lie. I've never had a man take me this way before.

He arched his eyebrows. "I keep thinking I've got humans figured out," he said, "but then you say some crazy shit like that, and I have to second guess."

Inspecting the chafe marks on my wrists, I replied, "Isn't it part of my job to keep you on your toes? At least until I lay you out."

"So I show you a real good time, and you still want to off me? That's how it is?" The questions had the lightness of humor behind them, but also a dark edge. He was sizing me up as a threat. We both knew it.

I lifted my gaze to meet his. "That's how it's always going to be."

The hardest part of my current situation was pretending not to think about Seth and Veronica alone together. The demon was, as I knew him, the consummate predator. In every other context, it had served me well. Now that I saw him directing his animal charm toward something of mine, I despised him for it.

As much as my mind wanted to dwell, however, Seth's intentions toward my gorgeous prize were neither here nor there. A significant percentage of the bear tribe lay dead, dying, or otherwise incapacitated in the other half of the bar, but my main targets, the vampires, had by and large regained themselves and were closing in around me. Keeping my wits sharp had never been more vital.

"What's the matter, old man?" I turned to the vampire brave enough to taunt me through a mouthful of broken teeth. He had obviously been a casualty of one of Seth's uninhibited pummelings, and yet his spirit seemed undaunted. "You look bothered. Couldn't be because your henchman ran off with the bitch, could it?"

"Watch your tongue, whelp." I enunciated each syllable with sharp precision, just to make it clear that the metaphorical ice beneath his feet was very thin. "If it's true my mood is less than charitable, then you ought to tread very lightly."

"Ha!" He coughed and spat on the floor. "Listen to yourself, *clanmaster*. As if you really think we're the ones who need to worry." He glanced to the left and right, at the unbecoming faces of his cohorts. Their circle around me drew ever tighter. "But that isn't the case, now is it?"

"I wouldn't be so sure." Logan had disappeared from sight, as was his wont, but I perceived him there, his frosted aura leaving a bite in the air. On my subtle signal, he stepped back into being at my side. The shadow of his fallen wings glimmered. Indulgently, I smiled at the intruders from Seattle. "What do you say we settle this? Right here, right now."

The answer did not come immediately. We stared each other down, unblinking. Droplets of blood fell from the vampire's chin to the filthy floor. Why they chose to hang out in such hovels, I had never understood.

At long last, he muttered, "Fine." The uneasy truce endured a few moments longer. Then, at the same time, we leapt forward. I struck him first, knocking his punch off its trajectory. His closed fist, quick, but smaller than mine, swooshed harmlessly past my face. Meanwhile, the cartilage in his nose shifted audibly beneath my knuckles.

He grunted and backpedaled, weaving. His left hand rose to cover his ruined features. A tooth bounced from his lower jaw off the ground.

"Cheap shot, you bastard." The narrowed eyes were yellowed and mean. "Should have known you wouldn't know how to fight fair."

"Come now." I offered my most infuriatingly ingratiating smile. "I won't apologize for your inability to hit me. That's ridiculous."

The eyes darkened with anger. He whirled on his back foot and charged forward again. This time, I side-stepped, allowing Logan to extend a deceptively impenetrable arm and clothesline him to the floor. The vamp lay flat on his back, all spirit drained from him. His gaze went glassy as he stared into Logan's face.

"Man, screw this!" a young, dark-skinned vamp cried out impatiently, galvanizing the small crowd. They surged forward to immerse us in hand-to-hand combat. Logan's first move was to open his ethereal wings, sending at least two enemies flying. He followed their flight arc all the way to where they hit the walls and fell.

While I admired the theatrics and the style of the fallen angel's method, mine stayed utilitarian. Quite a contrast to the usual flair for the dramatic, inherent in most of the more elegant creatures of the night, but try as I might, I couldn't scrub Seth and Veronica from my mind. Imagining my last glimpse of them as he led her off into the night made my insides churn.

I had to rejoin them as soon as possible. And that meant these weaklings were no more than useless obstacles.

But they had their own agenda on which they refused to give up, and they fought like madmen. I started off genuinely trying not to hurt them if I could help it, for as maddening as they were, the scope of the Seattle clan they came from far exceeded that of Anchorage. I needed to step carefully as clanmaster to avoid sinking my people into a trap we could not escape. Thus, the first vamp to stop cooperating in any fashion had his neck snapped.

A bold statement, but one that carried. The chaos around me paused in its intensity, long enough for the doomed vamp's associates to process what was going on. The downed vamp struggled to get away, but his body couldn't heal the damage I had done fast enough to save him. A broom handle taken from the closet and wielded with proper malintent spelled his doom.

Logan gave me an inscrutable, quiet look. If he had been a man of words, I figured he might have expressed some form of his differing opinion.

I understood at the same time that I didn't want to hear it. "Don't," I warned him, holding up a hand. "Now is not the time." More Seattleites seemed to be pouring out of the woodwork, rising up one behind the other like a shark's infinite rows of teeth. And they were not shy about attacking, trying to eliminate me for their own clanmaster to claim my territory.

At previous times in my life, there were some days when I absolutely felt the full centuries of my age. Some evenings, I woke up exhausted of it all.

Why couldn't my miserable, jackass rivals let me rule my slice of North America's wildest wilderness in peace? There was nothing up here that they could want except fish, real bears, and cold winters.

But the greed of a vampire knows no bounds. This was a truth I understood far too well. I, too, had fallen prey to extreme greed in my early days, back when I thought the game of survival in this wretched world was much more complicated.

Now I knew better. Our fight was beautiful in its cruel simplicity. It only had one rule, with no exceptions. And that was to survive.

The enemy flew at me, teeth gnashing, striking at the air with their unimpressive fists. Rarely did a punch connect, and when it did, I barely felt it. The only strength they had was in numbers. For some minutes, I could hardly see the room directly around me due to all the vamps advancing on my position. It should have been at least a fair fight, if not stacked against me and Logan. But the vamps held their ground with the same tenacity as paper dolls.

All too quickly, it became apparent that I could delegate the majority of the work to Logan. And so, I stood back, watching him throw them around as if they weren't beings of flesh at all. The oddity of the spectacle made me furrow my brow and think hard about the man who sent them—because he was not a stupid man.

Why were these the ones he had chosen to flock to Anchorage? Those who weren't weak were newcomers who stood no chance against any member of my clan. These unwelcome guests felt eerily dispensable, a whole army composed entirely of cannon fodder.

It was too easy. I had heard too many tales of the Seattle clanmaster to be fooled by a ruse of incompetence. Instinct warned me that he was using the bottom of his resources to gauge our strength. Not knowing the extent of his plans was enough to drive me mad.

"Tell me something." I had another vamp on his knees before me, glistening eyes wide and slowly filling with terror. This one was pitiable rather than detestable—not that that would buy him mercy. "Will your leader miss you when you have been ground to dust beneath my heel?"

The vamp's eyes darted unsteadily around the room. Anywhere but meeting my gaze. I palmed the broom handle that I had used to kill several of his associates and nailed him in the head with it.

The noise it made on impact with his skull suggested hollowness between his ears.

"Speak," I told him calmly. "Now."

The vampire started to laugh nervously. The high pitched, atonal melody of his manic giggles cut through the air. Logan frowned in his direction, and so did I.

"The boss is coming for you," he declared. "No matter what. We're only the beginning. And when he gets here…" The laughter reached a fever pitch. He wrapped his sinewy arms around himself and rocked back and forth. "I'd leave it empty for him if I were you. Otherwise…" He shook his head. "Boss has no problem scorching the earth. He knows he can always rebuild."

I clenched my teeth. "I'll scorch it myself before I let him take it."

"Doesn't matter," said the vampire again. "He'll be happy to take it anyway." Once more, the laughter swelled, as did the rage inside me. I blinked, and when I opened my eyes, the broom handle was embedded in the center of the vamp's chest. He fell backwards, nearly in half. His eyes had become fixed on death.

But his last words stuck with me unpleasantly.

*He'll be happy to take it anyway.*

Well, I was more than ready to see him try.

The shrill wail of sirens cut through the air: our signal that time was running short. Logan caught my eye across the room, and we both headed for the closest exit. Not all the vamps and bears were dead, but that was all right. They'd look like humans again by the time the cops busted their way in, and we'd be long gone.

On my way out the back, I glanced toward the splashing of red and blue as it tore down the street behind me. At first, only one patrol unit showed up to the scene, and I contemplated sticking around for a while to keep an eye on their activities. Then a whole caravan of others materialized at the end of the road.

Quietly, I melted into the shadows. Observation would have to be another day. Secretly, I was relieved, because it meant I could separate Seth and Veronica faster.

But that relief didn't last beyond the first step through the door. I smelled it immediately, that unique aroma I knew so well. Musk, and sweat, and the scent of a woman, mixed with the demon's sickening stench of brimstone.

At that moment, he appeared at the top of the staircase. I knew I was too late. He had already done that for which I had privately sworn to destroy him. And Veronica was somewhere up there—even still in his bed—tainted. Deflowered by a demon.

"You are a dead man, Seth," I whispered.

# CHAPTER 16

## LOGAN

I could hear Orion and Seth shouting up on the next floor. Nothing new about that—it hardly ever took long for them to be at each other's throats. But this was a new record even for them. Orion had barely been inside the front door before the chaos began. And from the sounds of it, the show wasn't stopping anytime soon.

"Why don't you kill me, then?" Seth roared. "Seems like you want to, so come on! You know I never turn down a fight!" He laughed, and then a shattering crash shook the house's frame. I wondered what kind of scene I might find the next time I walked through the upper floor. It wouldn't be the first time one of their skirmishes had torn the place apart.

If Orion was dignifying Seth's outbursts with responses, I couldn't hear them. His anger took a different shape than the demon's, perhaps unsurprisingly. Orion's rage was more like mine: quiet, seething, and running deep. Though the two were temporary allies, they had never been friends. I thought the likelihood of them eventually parting on benevolent terms was slim to none.

Another crash rattled the window. Seth laughed again. I could see him in my mind's eye, head thrown back, grinning mouth ajar. He delighted in this type of discord for discord's sake. Never was he happier than when Orion was pissed. And this time, Orion was *pissed.*

I knew why, of course. Anyone with eyes in their head could have deduced the way he felt about the girl with the pink hair. Before that night, he hadn't ever struck me as the type to keep those kinds of trophies, but there was no denying that he saw something in her.

Was it the same hazy familiarity I had seen in the moments prior to bringing her forward? The thought that Orion and I might have more in common never crossed my mind. I was uninterested in him, aside from our working relationship, and as far as I knew, the feeling was mutual. But we had this mutual curiosity about the girl.

Normally, if push came to shove, I'd be the one to back down without question. It was rarely a good idea to get on Orion's bad side, and after all the time and effort I'd already invested in his endeavors, I was committed to seeing things through. A moment of hollow triumph simply wasn't worth the risk of loss.

The entrance of the mysterious girl had changed my perspective, however. Her presence awakened a long-dormant curiosity the likes of which I had long since assumed I would never feel again. She made me dive reluctantly down into my past and bring up memories from those depths. Memories of a time less dark and barren.

Ironically, they were the same memories Orion had tapped to secure my pledge of temporary loyalty. Now they both seized upon that hidden longing, the ache of regret. In her bright, pretty face, I saw the life I had lost in order to gain the burden of the wings upon my back.

It was stupid to believe she could grant me a wish that I'd already taken on an enormous debt to fulfill. And yet I couldn't seem to help myself. I wanted to see her again. Her aura haunted me.

Out of the corner of my eye, I caught a blur of movement out in the hallway and turned to see the door to the room I was in swinging wider. There she stood, as if a vision manifested by the call of my desires. Skin-tight pants, thick coat that remained unbuttoned to reveal a gray simple top, and unruly pink hair draped over her shoulders. But those gorgeous eyes carried so many emotions. Fear. Confusion. Anger.

I blinked. She blinked. We stared dumbly into each other's eyes for a few moments longer than necessary.

"Oh my God. I didn't see you in here." She spoke suddenly. The puzzled clouds in her eyes cleared. She shook her head. "I'm sorry. I thought this was...actually, I don't know what I thought this was. The bathroom?" An apologetic little smile tilted her lip, then immediately faded in the face of another booming impact from upstairs of our large home. The ceiling trembled.

"The bathroom is there." I nodded to the opposite wall, where another door led out. "If that's what you need."

It wasn't what she had been looking for. We

both knew that. My best assumption was that she had really been searching for a way out that might protect her from Orion's keen perception. Her gaze darted toward the window, more or less confirming my thoughts.

"Come on!" Seth bellowed again from the floor above. He guffawed. The sound was becoming a regular refrain that I expected to keep up for some time yet. When those two really got going, they could trade hits for hours. And still, no matter how hard I listened, Orion remained inaudible. His anger, on the other hand, seeped through the entire house. It was almost tangible, a smothering haze.

The girl rolled her eyes. "I can't believe them. Honestly, I can't believe *this*." She opened her mouth to continue, changed her mind, and closed it again, pressing her lips into a thin line. Then she just looked at me.

I said, "You can hide out in here until they're done. I don't care. But it might be a while." The silvery splintering of glass supported my statement. I shrugged. "See?"

She took a deep breath. I watched her lungs fill and deflate, her heartbeat slowing. One hand wandered through her mane of messy pink waves, the other wrapped like a security blanket around her own waist. "I guess this happens pretty often, huh?"

"They were getting better," I admitted. "Don't think that's the case anymore."

"Ugh." She sat down heavily on the end of the couch and balled her fists up in the cushion. "I'm sorry. I don't know how you stand living here."

"You say that like you don't assume this is where I belong." I kept my eyes on her. How much was she able to work out about me, about who I was? How far could she see into the nature of my spirit? These were questions I hadn't bothered to ask about anyone before. None had mattered before her. But suddenly I was hungry for—what? Gratification, perhaps. Or in a strange, abhorrent way…approval?

She paused long enough to take another breath and weigh her response. "My name is Veronica," she said at last. "In case you forgot from the last time we met."

Somehow it made sense to me that she'd been given a devoutly religious name, despite, or maybe because of, the utter profanity of her chosen profession. She had the look of a modern saint, inner strength cloaked in a shroud of innocence.

The hue of her hair was a strange, befitting touch. Highlighted by gentle beams of moonlight, it held a pale glow.

"I'm Logan," I told her. "Orion calls me Logan."

"And what about Seth?" she asked dryly.

I chuckled. "He doesn't call me anything." Not quite true. He had a whole repertoire of irritating nicknames. The only one I had ever heard him consistently calling by name was Orion, and then only because he knew he was required to show a modicum of respect in order to get what he had been promised.

"I like Logan," Veronica responded, glancing up to the shaking ceiling. "It suits you." She turned to face me. Her shoes were untied, the laces dragging along the floor. Clearly she'd dressed in a hurry. "What are you doing here, Logan?" she asked now. "To answer your question, no. I don't think you really belong here. If you did, you'd be upstairs slugging it out with Beavis and Butthead."

"I could be." I caught her uncertain gaze and held it.

"But...?" I asked. Her tenacious personality shone through in every exchange. Veronica thought I had secrets she might want or need to know which explained why she hadn't turned and walked out of the house. And she was determined to get answers out of me, I saw it in her narrowing gaze. That was annoying, but for reasons I didn't quite understand, I decided to indulge her. To push her away would be to stunt the growth of a tempting connection.

"Not worth my time." I frowned and glanced at the ceiling. Another rattling blow shook the building to its foundation. A hint of brimstone smoke filtered down to us through the staircase. Apparently Seth had doubled down, as he often did.

Veronica noticed the smoke as well. "Is everything okay up there?" For a brief moment, nervousness flashed across her face. "He's not going to send this place up, is he?" She laid a hand on the wall, feeling for heat.

I shook my head. "There's too much at stake for that."

"Good to know, I think." She stepped toward me until we were less than a few feet apart. Her presence had a tangible warmth, in stark contrast to mine. She was the sun on the surface of a frozen lake too deep and cold to melt. But she was trying. And I had to admit it was making more difference than none at all. "Tell me what Orion's got on you.

Maybe I can help. Why else would you be working with him, right?"

I frowned once more. "No, and no. You can't."

She folded her arms. Stubbornness radiated off of her in waves. Veronica wasn't going anywhere. "Try me," she declared flatly. "Really. I dare you. I'm stronger than you all seem to think."

"Are you?" I rounded on her then. Not to hurt or scare her so much as to teach her a lesson. She was correct about her strength; that much I could feel. But for all her potential, all her current capability, the girl was stunningly naïve. There were occasions in which her forthright, persistent manner might get her somewhere.

More often than not, it would come back to bite her. Hard.

"You're mistaken to think there's always going to be a place for you in these conflicts." My voice was calm, but dark. "We don't have the patience to entertain the meaningless designs of mortals." Quick as a flash, I reached out and grasped her slender wrist.

She tensed.

I turned her arm over, tracing the blue lines of her veins with my finger and pressing down until her pulse thrummed beneath my touch. "Do you know what this is?" I asked her.

She stared at me in silence. Her large, luminous eyes stayed impressively inscrutable. Eventually, she moved her head the tiniest amount left and right.

I didn't let her look away. "It's a timer. And it's counting down."

ogan's hands were cold, but his touch was softer than I expected. His silver-blue eyes, eerily light, bored into mine, his ash-gray hair sitting on his shoulders. Part of me wanted to back away and free myself from the otherworldly grip he had on me, but another, larger part remained a somewhat willing captive. Besides, I didn't think he really meant to hurt me—not in the moment, at least. No doubt he could have removed himself from service with Orion and Seth just as he claimed. And he'd even caught me off guard.

I knew I was being reckless as hell, trying to coax him into opening up. And I knew it was cliché to think he wasn't like the other supernaturals I had seen. The voice of reason inside my head did her best to persuade me otherwise. *Are you nuts, Veronica? Can you hear yourself thinking right now? This guy is not a neglected puppy locked up in a back room. He's strong, and he's smart, and he's definitely more dangerous than he looks!*

All true. I understood it in my heart. Still, Logan was the only one I had found myself able to talk to as if we were almost equals. He was moody, sure, and obviously capable of great cruelty. But he lacked the arrogance of his compatriots. He spoke without their repulsive smugness. I nearly believed he thought he might not actually be better than me.

Though, there was so much to him I had to uncover. I wanted to know about that secret core, lurking like the shadow of a leviathan below the surface of the water. There were so many mysteries I had yet to unlock. And he was one I understood the least.

"Talking about death isn't going to scare me," I informed him now. "Look, I don't know how much experience you really have with vamps, but they're not very nice. I'm..." I hesitated on the brink of spilling that I was from the Pacific Northwest—in fact, the very same city that harbored Orion's rivals. What he'd do with that knowledge was utterly unpredictable. He could use it against me. He could throw me to the wolves. "I've seen some pretty awful shit."

Dylan's face, a guy I'd been dating and lost to a vamp assault when I was seventeen, floated up into the back of my mind, and I tried to keep my face as neutral as possible. Logan paused and looked at me, suddenly curious. His fingertips moved lightly along the inside of my arm, as if he was reading the path of my veins.

"Who is that?" he asked quietly. The intensity of his stare chilled me deeply. I knew he had to be talking about Dylan, even though it didn't make sense. Had he seen my recollections of him? "Lost," Logan added, more or less to himself.

I chewed on my lower lip. Abruptly, the situation in this room had turned intimate in a weird, intangible way. I felt like the tables were turning on me; I was no longer the one doing the prying. And on one hand, that made me extremely uncomfortable. Dylan was, to me, a rather sacred subject, though I haven't thought of him in a while. I pushed the tragedy to the farthest recesses of my mind. Even thinking about him for too long made my eyes sting.

"He died." Those two words were all I could

manage at first. I had no idea why they felt so different to say in front of this silent stranger. "They killed him," I finished at length. "The vamps. Okay? Is that what you wanted?"

Why was I the one being interrogated now, and how had he done it without saying more than a few words? He was still gazing at me with that X-ray vision, his eyes like marble glaciers.

"You hold it against them," he murmured. "I see."

"Yeah. Yeah, of course I do," I blurted. "They fucking murdered my friend!" A slow wave of heat crept up through my chest and neck, coloring my cheeks. This was a pain I had not expected to revisit when I stepped through the door, and for a minute, I truly regretted it. Dylan was my secret, my own private knot of pain to carry, and suddenly it was all out in the open again. The wounds that had not fully healed squeezed out a few drops of fresh blood.

"So you hunt them for what? Vengeance?" The twist of amusement in his smooth, cool voice raised my hackles.

I curled my fingers into a fist against his palm and yanked my hand away.

He let me go easily, unperturbed. I'd have been

lying if I said I didn't think about hitting him right in his perfectly chiseled, Adonis-y face. Then the white-hot flash of anger died down.

*Breathe, girl.* I tossed my hair defiantly. Taking my wrist back made me realize that it was numb and freezing. Alarmed, I tried to shake some feeling back into my extremities. "Hey, what the hell did you do to my hand?"

"Sorry," he remarked nonchalantly. "Side effect. It will go away."

"Ugh." I scowled at him. "You know, I didn't give you permission. For any of that."

Logan remained totally unconcerned. He leaned back against the wall of the window alcove where he was sitting, propping one foot up on the edge of the window seat. "Death is public domain," he said.

"But my memories aren't. And before you go denying anything, I know you saw something, because that's the only way you could've known about Dylan. Thanks for bringing him up, by the way. That's exactly what I needed today." As I finished the last sentence, I realized with a start how panicked I was. Both my heart and my thoughts raced a million miles a minute as I attempted to collect myself. Tears gathered at the corners of my eyes. "Don't ever do that again."

Logan observed me without a word. Then he reached out. "Give me back your hand."

"No." I shook my head. My hair fell into my face, and I pushed it fiercely back. Distraught or not, there was not going to be any hiding. I was just trying not to remember the way Dylan looked when I found him. "Don't touch me."

He gave me a slightly impatient look, as if I were simply being difficult instead of having a panic attack. "Is that why you think you can 'help' me?" His tone was disarmingly conversational. "Because you think your vendetta against Orion and his kind means we have something in common? Or is it that something else stirs in your veins?"

"It's not a vendetta, and what do you mean?" Having a point to argue forced me to focus and cleared some of the fog from my brain. "They have no place here among mortals. All they do is spread chaos and kill." A lump rose in my throat. I swallowed hard. "I'm not the only one who thinks they're a plague. Therefore, not a vendetta."

"If you say so." He caught my eye once more, and I was startled to see that he'd reclaimed my hand without me noticing. His fingertips resumed their delicate, precise track over my skin. "You never answered the first question."

"Do I have to? You never answered mine either." I was unapologetically sullen. He had gotten me more out of sorts than I wanted to admit.

"I would appreciate if you answered. And there's nothing for me to reveal about you, other than I sense something unusual. But I don't know what it is." The way he talked was so bafflingly unassuming, for a man who kept the company he did. Upstairs, the battle raged on between his two untamed associates. Every now and then I caught another whiff of Seth's smoke, usually right around the same time as another thing hit the ceiling. The house trembled intermittently at the center of its own personal earthquake.

"Fine." I tugged at my arm, but he held fast. "Move over, then," I grumbled. "If you're going to keep me trapped, the least you can do is give me a seat." Logan moved his foot, and I sat down in the newly available space on the couch. "I don't know why I offered to help you. Not like you're asking for any. I think I just...thought you were different in some way."

Hearing the words leave my mouth made me cringe internally. What was I still doing in this room, talking to this guy? Being near him was like being hypnotized but self-aware. I knew full well that he was having an unanticipated effect on me, and that my efforts to resist weren't entirely successful. The source of Logan's allure wasn't as readily apparent as with Orion or Seth, either, although he was just as handsome.

I had always been drawn harder to men whose first instincts were to issue orders or start fights. Logan exuded a different type of power and charisma. He preferred to bide his time, waiting patiently in the shadows for the right moment to strike.

He ran the side of his index finger along the length of my forearm, smiling slightly as goosebumps raised on my skin. "I am…unique," he said slowly. "But it doesn't matter. There is no help for the fallen."

I furrowed my brow. "Fallen from where?"

"Grace." He shrugged his shoulders. "Paradise. Whatever you want to call it. I was there, and now I'm here, and there is nothing to be done."

I froze, my mouth dropping open at first. "No way." Throughout my time in the field, I'd heard of certain forsaken beings, but not in any concrete sense. The rumors of things like cursed angels held the quality of urban legends, so rare were the shreds of proof. Up until I realized that Logan was very serious, I wasn't sure I believed them at all.

Logan, for his part, could not have cared less whether I subscribed to his reality or not. He idly spread my fingers apart, traced over the lines in my palm, and let me go. "I'm not going to convince you." The trace of irritation crept back into his tone. "You're too raw and idealistic. I would suggest you come back to discuss your experiences in a hundred years, but you'll be dead by then."

"Wow, okay. Sorry I asked." Now he was the one acting sullen and difficult, and some of his mysterious charm was wearing off. "I was just trying to..." I trailed off. "Actually, I have no idea what I was trying to do."

Just then, Logan held a finger to his lips. "Shh." I shut my mouth and we both listened together—to brand new, total quiet. The cacophony in the background had faded to a dull roar the longer it had gone on. It was a mild shock to recognize that I heard nothing.

"They're done," Logan said. "You have to go. Unless you want Orion to find you in here."

"No thanks," I retorted wryly. "Sounds like he's already trashed the place. I don't need him to snap me in half for good measure."

Logan studied me closely. "You shouldn't have come here," he said. The sentiment was both sudden and unprompted.

"I didn't. Seth brought me because Orion told him to."

"No," he said. "To Anchorage."

"Oh." I laughed. "Well, it's too late for that. I only had a one-way ticket." I thought I was being funny, but Logan's face remained unmoved. He was so stoic, so carefully measured in all ways. The unnatural perfection of his features made him seem like a living statue, framed by the arch of the window.

Shit, maybe he was an angel after all. The shock rattled through me. I was used to bumping into different supernatural creatures, but an angel was a first. Fallen angel for that, still as startling. So, what was he doing down on Earth?

A sudden sharp bang yanked me back into the real world, and I glanced into the hall, toward the stairwell. One last thin current of smoke drifted in through the open door.

"Seth is leaving," Logan remarked. He pointed

down from our vantage point in the window, to where Seth was just being swallowed up by the thick trees. Watery footprints marked his trail from the house to the edge of the wood. "Fight's over."

"I guess that's my cue to get moving." I stood up, moved away from the window seat, paused, and glanced back at him. "Can't say I blame you staying away from Seth, though. I don't really want to fight him either."

"The fighting isn't the problem." Logan's face masked over into stony resolve. "I don't want to kill him. Yet."

I was out of the living room pretty quickly after that. The more I learned about this house, the more it seemed like a constant power struggle between three personalities that were each dominant in their own way. Orion, the ironclad leader, Seth, the wild enforcer, and Logan, the patient strategist. It was a house of cards, built precariously on the foundation of impermanent loyalties.

And I had arrived just in time to watch it all start to give way.

# CHAPTER 18

## ORION

Every fight with Seth forced me to remember two things. One, he was not like the vampires I had bullied into loyalty to me, and to mentally categorize him as such was a mistake. Two, the surrender of mortal life did not necessarily mean the absence of pain. I stood under the showerhead, wincing as the burns on my arms and chest shed off and began the process of healing over. A process I was simultaneously thankful for and disgusted by.

In the end, I stepped out from under the water without permanent wounds. By the next nightfall, there would be no sign of an altercation. This was hardly the first time our tempers had risen to their flashpoint. I knew it wouldn't be the last. The encounters had taken on their own ritualistic vibe, a way for us to release the constantly mounting pressure day by day. If Seth respected anything, I liked to think it was my willingness to engage with him in my arena.

He wanted to fight, so we fought. And I let him think he could get the better of me, that he was calling the shots. These battles always ended on one side of a very thin line, and I didn't expect to see hide nor hair of the demon for a while. But Seth was greedy above all else, and I had promised too rich a reward. The siren song of wealth and freedom always drew him back.

But after each battle we engaged, something changed with us… only minuscule, but the wall between us always thinned. By meeting him on his grounds of how he dealt with problems, I believed he started to come around to working closer with me.

So, I embraced our encounters, knowing it aided us both to deal with the shit between us. I didn't want to constantly argue with him or to have him endlessly piss me off. These small steps were progress as far as I was concerned.

As I toweled myself dry, I glanced in the mirror, briefly contemplating the figure I saw there. An old soul corralled into a comparatively young body for eternity…if all went according to plan. I barely remembered what it was like to be mortal in this suit of flesh, to feel the warm blood running through my veins. Had I lived more richly due to the impermanence of it all?

My reflection and I smiled at each other. No, of course not. What a foolish notion. The two greatest enemies of the mortal man were time and death. I had conquered both. Now my foes were strictly tangible, not concepts hiding out in the furthest corners of my mind. And that meant they could all be soundly defeated.

The house, being old and drafty, had a distinct, salty chill when the sun was down. I preferred it, personally, and on occasion I retired entirely devoid of clothing. The sensation of settling into cool, grainy soil was one I had taken a long time to embrace—it was hard to process how much the meaning of a grave had changed after turning. But on this night, rest had to wait. I slipped into some clothes—wincing at the sting of newly forming raw skin rubbing against cloth—and retraced my steps downstairs.

The aftermath of our latest brawl was impressive, in its own uncivilized way. The floor was littered with shards of glass, some of which had melted into iridescent disks on the floor. Most of the cabinet doors in the kitchen hung open, their contents either strewn about or simply broken. The refrigerator, which none of us used much anyway, no longer hummed; it and the stove had been marred by a scorch mark that splashed across the back wall as well.

I couldn't help but be amused. Were we no better than a pair of squabbling children fighting over a toy? But even as I had the thought, I understood the depth of my investment. However much I indulged Seth's wildness normally, my anger had been a lot more real than usual. I had found a flower, and he had plucked off the bloom.

Not that it mattered at the moment. He had gone off alone, and the house was still a mess. If not for my attention to image, I might have been happy to leave the second floor in ruins. But the Seattle clan still had their eyes on me. It wouldn't do to have my personal dwelling fall to pieces.

The footfalls pattered down the corridor behind me as I swept up the debris on the tile. I recognized her before she spoke a word; in fact, I had felt her moving toward me.

"Orion?" She said my name cautiously, as if she

thought it might summon someone other than me. Or perhaps bearing partial witness to my dust-up with Seth had convinced her to fear me.

"What do you want?" I asked her tersely. "Did Seth leave you wanting?"

She frowned at my back when I glanced behind me. "Don't be a prick. I just came to check on you."

I shot her a derisive glance, but she was already examining the state of the kitchen and the living room beyond. "Feel free to atone for your pleasure in any way you see fit." As a tactful suggestion, I took a washrag from the sink and tossed it over my shoulder at her.

She stepped toward me. "I'm sorry. I didn't realize we had any kind of deal at all, let alone an exclusive one." There was a pause. "I also didn't realize I'd be cleaning your house for free." On her way past me, she looked me over in what I assumed was supposed to be a disdainful way. Then her eyes flicked over the exposed burns on my neck and arms, and she stopped. "Hey, wait. You're hurt."

"And you expect me to believe this concerns you?" I laughed. "Don't mock me, Veronica. I have no need for your pity."

"Ugh. Let me see your arm."

I eyed her closely. "Most kidnapping victims wouldn't go out of their way to aid their captor."

"Well, you haven't killed me yet," she quipped. Then she said, "Judging by the dents you made in the sheetrock here, I figure you're not just mad at Seth."

Hearing his name in her voice made me bristle. Veronica felt the tension and paused. "You should wrap that."

"It's unnecessary," I told her. "In a matter of hours, these injuries will be gone. They mean nothing."

"Yes, I'm aware of how vampire regeneration works, thank you." She raised an eyebrow. "That's why it's so goddamn hard to get one of you to stay down for good."

Her hands were warm on my skin, life radiating from her touch. I let the faint drum of her heartbeat invade my ears and thought about how perfect she would be if I could wrest her from the unforgiving clutches of time, as I had been. Her pale skin, a shade paler. Her beauty preserved for all eternity. And of course, the mark of her sire somewhere on her body.

She had retrieved a rag, wet it under the faucet, and brought it back to me. I blinked, suddenly aware of how near she was. She moved up my arm toward the cutoff of my shirtsleeve. The cool water was, admittedly, quite soothing on the burn. "But then again," she continued, "here you are in a bachelor pad with two other guys. That's not what I would've expected out of a clanmaster either."

Had the words come from anyone else, I might have been offended, perhaps deeply. But Veronica spoke with such open candor that I found it impossible to rebuke her. She barely entertained the thought of a lie.

"I would be interested to know whoever you thought you were going to meet by coming here," I said. "And what you hoped to accomplish? Anchorage is not a city for outsiders."

Veronica gave me a look, her eyes sparkling. "Who said I was an outsider, Orion? Maybe you just didn't know me before."

I shook my head. "No. I would remember you." An insolent beauty like hers would never have left me until I captured it for good.

She scoffed. "Well, whatever I thought I was looking for, it sure wasn't…" She gestured vaguely around at the house. "This."

Once more we lapsed into a comfortable silence. Veronica pulled the shirt from my shoulder to apply the next compress. I hissed a breath through my teeth as the cloth made contact. "Infernal demonic mutt," I muttered.

"Says the guy regularly putting up with him." Veronica gave me a sidelong glance. "Honestly, help me if I'm missing something. You *despise* this guy, don't you?"

"It's none of your business, but since you are currently providing a service, I might be inclined to entertain your questions." Running a hand through my hair, I sighed. *What are you doing, Orion? She's just a nosy little girl. She could use this against you.* In my soul, I knew I was letting a foolish, blinding desire get the better of my common sense.

Nevertheless, an unquenchable yearning smoldered within me. Her gaze flicked to mine, igniting the endless fuse. She smirked. "You vamps always look so tortured. Must be hard, living forever and trying not to get stabbed through the heart."

It was my turn to scowl. I grunted out a reply. "The demon is helping me protect my clan, and despite how it looks, not to mention how much he does piss me off, underneath his fiery demeanor, I see someone who reminds me of myself."

His admission surprised me. "How so?"

"That's something you can work out on your own."

She eyed me with narrowing eyes. "That I will. And to answer your earlier comment about exclusivity, I don't belong to you, Orion. I belong to whom I give permission to, be it one or three men." She held my gaze to drive her point across.

Her words swirled on my mind, and I stiffened in my seat, unsure how to respond. She'd been eyeing Logan too? I bit back my initial response to counter her comment. Sharing wasn't in my nature, but I also suspected her being forced into anything wasn't in hers.

"What exactly are you hoping to achieve in town then?" I asked.

She finished up with the last of the compresses, returned to the sink, and washed her hands. "We both know I'm not here to protect you or your people." Her slender arms folded sternly across her chest, changing the topic. "Quite the opposite, actually."

I glowered at her. "Your intentions are a thorn in my side, and yet, you're far from the biggest threat. There are others attempting to invade the territory and steal it from its rightful heirs." I stared at her. "I will kill anyone who tries."

"Like the guy you threw in the river," she said.

I shrugged. "Casualties are an inevitable possibility. He knew where he could end up once he set foot in my city. I make no apologies for defending the clan's right to our land."

The expression on Veronica's exquisite face shifted between exasperation and something else that I couldn't quite pinpoint. Eventually, the frustration won, and she pinched the bridge of her nose, squeezing her eyes shut. "That may be…but you're still murdering people, Orion. Violence always brings about collateral damage sooner or later. Someone totally innocent is going to die because of this."

"So be it." I let my gaze roam over her body. "Your kind was meant to be sacrificed."

"You just lost all the points I was willing to give you for sparing my life." She tossed her hair. "I'm gonna go ahead and say you broke even at a big, fat zero."

I grinned. "A harsh judgment, but perhaps it is fair." One of the compresses threatened to slide off my arm, and when she turned her attention to straightening it, I reached out with the other arm and caught her by the waist. Immediately, her knuckles dug into my chest, close to another hidden spot where Seth had left burns.

The pain I would have felt was completely overshadowed by the thrill of touching her. She braced against me, her taut muscles coiled. "Let go."

"I will." I spoke in a low, almost gentle voice, directly into her ear. "What's more, I won't even harm a hair on your gorgeous head. But if you think you'll be out of my sight for long ever again from this point forward, I have bad news for you, my darling."

"Watch yourself," she warned. Her fingers curled into a fist. "I'm not afraid of you."

"Maybe not now," I murmured. "But I think you could learn."

# CHAPTER 19

## LOGAN

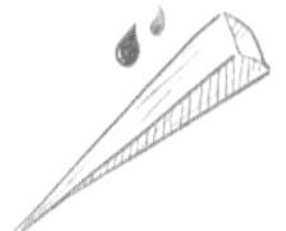

As unabashedly bitter as I had become, I had never learned to revel in the brutal glories of conflict quite like Seth and Orion. Their latest fight cast a heavy pall over the house, the air thick with unspoken tension that made my skin crawl. For perhaps the first time, I started to feel the restraints of the mortal plane quite acutely.

When my allies were fighting like a pair of spoiled children, it was hard to know if I had truly made the best choice. The days remained largely unchanged, as Orion lay dormant in his makeshift grave during the day and either dealing with the enemies or watching over Veronica at night, while Seth disappeared somewhere. But each emerged fully reinvigorated, self-righteous tempers ready to flare.

I sat by the window and listened for the sound of one or both of them leaving. Only then would I be able to recapture an echo of the serenity I'd grown accustomed to. And even still, the threat of their return cast an enormous shadow over any hope of peace. How foolish I had been to take the quiet, uneventful days for granted!

We were all on edge. Seth in particular seemed to sense my displeasure—and held it against me. On the rare occasion that our paths happened to cross in the house, he stared me down, eyes narrow. I bore the brunt of his suspicious passive aggression for a matter of days, maybe a week. Then I couldn't take it anymore.

The demon shouldered past me in the upstairs hallway. His gaze clashed with mine. "What?" I snapped, almost before I had the chance to realize what I was saying. We stopped at the same time, turning to face each other. "Do you have a problem, Seth? Because now is the time to air your grievances."

He looked at me and arched an eyebrow. "Well, well, well, Logan. And here I thought you didn't have an ounce of fire in you." A condescending smirk lifted his lip. "I've gotta say, I'm impressed."

"Don't be. I don't care." I glared steadily into his face. "Are we going to talk, or is this a waste of time?"

"Listen, angel boy." His retort was sharp and immediate. "No idea what the fuck's gotten into you, but since we're already here, I'll lay it out. This little Three Musketeers act Orion thinks he has going isn't gonna hold up too much longer, so you need to decide what side of the line you'll be on when the shit hits the fan."

I chuckled. "I guess you think you're going to kill him."

Seth glowered. "Who's going to stop me if I do?" He stepped closer. "I won't pretend I know anything about what's going on in your head. But I'm telling you right now, you're not a match for me. Not even close."

"That's not true," I said calmly. "You're kidding yourself if you don't think one of the reasons I'm here is because Orion knows I can put you down." I didn't say it would be a tall order to do so, or that I knew better than to imagine I'd come out unscathed.

Seth's composure slipped just long enough to

expose the bubbling chasm of rage within. His irises blackened, his expression hardening into a mask of dark fury. The air around his body shimmered with a searing burst of heat that I could feel from where I stood. In the next moment, he was inches from my face. "Watch your step, Logan," he growled. "It's a fucking long way down."

This close, he reeked of hell and alcohol, and the veins in his face and neck threatened to pop. Despite the way in which he constantly sought to pave a pathway to ruin, by any means necessary, I found his existence grotesquely fascinating. A being made of little more than self-indulgent passions, barely contained in corporeal form. Really, we were lucky he hadn't self-destructed long ago.

I laughed at him. "Look at you, presuming to talk to me about falling. That's very funny, Seth." I paused. "I recommend you save your breath. Someday soon you might not have any more to waste."

If looks could kill, I would have dropped right where I stood. He turned and stormed away toward his room down the hall, leaving me to be washed over by his searing wake. The slamming of his door sent a tremor down through the foundation.

Technically, by standing firm, I had come out on top. But I didn't wait around to see if he'd reemerge looking for a second round. It was my turn to retreat into my own modest sanctuary—not that a closed door provided much protection from Seth's ire. Still, I made sure to engage the lock.

It was all becoming too much to handle. Homesickness wasn't an emotion I'd ever felt in regard to the underworld, the cold, cruel side of the veil between dimensions, and yet I longed to step back into that blessedly serene realm for a little while. The barren plains of stone and ice would be a balm to my senses.

Orion wouldn't like it; that much I understood implicitly. He wouldn't like it, but he lacked the authority to prevent me from returning to my place of origin. And I was coming back. I just needed a respite from this chaotic space and the people with whom I had to share it.

A floor above, Orion slept in his modern crypt, dead to the world. I had learned from experience how difficult it was to rouse him from that state, but I kept my guard up nonetheless. If he should happen upon me while I was transitioning back and forth between realms, I'd be too vulnerable for comfort.

But as it turned out, none of that mattered. After I settled down to begin the rite of passage, I was quickly met by a strange sense of emptiness, as if looking off the edge of a broken-down road into nothingness. Where the path to the underworld should have manifested before me, I instead saw nothing more than dense, immaterial fog. And when I attempted to walk forward through the veil between dimensions, the haze cleared to reveal a solid barrier.

Something wasn't right. Confused, I walked along the wall, running a hand over its smooth, unyielding surface. No door opened to admit me, no gateway broke free to let me through. Not even my wings could carry me over.

I was locked out. In disbelief, I stared at the cursed obstacle, mulling it over in my mind for much longer than was necessary. There had to be a way through, or around, or behind. Not once in the considerable time I'd spent moving between realms had the path ever closed without my knowledge. I felt a stone forming in the pit of my stomach.

Could it be that the paths had been altered somehow? The thought of some rogue supernatural tampering with gates between the planes filled me with unease. I knew of no one with the audacity, let alone the power. And worse, the only other person who might have more information was the very individual I'd intended to avoid for the foreseeable future—Seth.

I closed my eyes, and when I opened them, I was sitting on the side of my bed in Orion's house. The light vertigo that always accompanied any planar shifting caused the world to rock gently for a few seconds. I shook it off and pushed to my feet. Best to get this conversation over with while Orion was still unconscious. No doubt he would want to be consulted, but these were not matters to be presided over by an ex-mortal.

I walked down the long hall, focusing my gaze straight ahead on the entrance to Seth's room. At first, my knock received no answer. Then he was standing in the doorway, leaning on the frame, staring at me.

"Screw off," he said. He took a deep breath and the next words he spoke were heavy with sullen resentment. "What do you want?"

I chose not to mince words. "I can't go back."

"Huh?" The momentary confusion in his expression morphed quickly into amusement at my expense. "So they changed the locks on you, huh? And what, you want me to see if I can get you in my way?"

I shook my head. "The way is blocked. I think there's something wrong." My assumption was, of course, that Seth would both understand and care about how a problem beyond the veil might affect him. In hindsight, I should have known better. He was a creature of almost pure impulse, for whom the past and the future meant equally little.

Seth shrugged. "Sounds like you've been kicked out," he remarked. "Hate to be the bearer of bad news, but you know how it is in those shitholes. You start the wrong fight, you commit the wrong murder, you get on the wrong bad side, and that's it. You're out until you can weasel your way back in." He stepped back into his room, preparing to close the door. "Tough luck, angel boy. Maybe you can try again in a couple hundred years."

"No." I caught the door and held it. "This is different."

"Could be." Seth frowned. "Either way, not my problem. You said you're tough, so figure it out." With that, he forced the door shut. I heard the lock click into place. Once more, silence reigned in the house. And I was on my own.

Having been denied my preferred method of escape, I decided to take the next best option: a walk around the city. Anchorage's unique blend of desolation and wild beauty often helped to clear my mind, and I needed the fresh air. But as I made my way down the winding drive toward the road, all illusion of the peaceful, meditative walk I had envisioned rushed from my mind.

Something else took up residence there—an explosion of bloody violence, a primal scream of unsophisticated rage. Almost unconsciously, I turned toward the source and broke into a run, wings unfurling. Seconds later, the wind caught their edge, and I began to ascend.

I was back in my room at the Anchorage Grand Hotel before the night's events really hit me. Suddenly drained, and more than a little sore, I stepped into a long, hot shower to scrub off my sins and think about what I'd just done. As wild as I'd expected my night to get, screwing a demon was one thing that had absolutely not been on my radar. And yet…there I was, steamy water pouring over me, flashbacks from that night filling my mind's eye.

"God damn it, Veronica," I muttered. Ever since Dylan's death, my cardinal rule had been not to get involved with the subjects of my investigations. Such emotional investment was just asking for trouble. Hell, I'd seen it happen to other people in front of my eyes and openly criticized them for it.

Dylan and I first fell for each other when I was sixteen and he was nineteen. It happened at the height of the vamp wars in Seattle, when he fought to keep streets safe, to cease the constant battles between vampire clans. I adored his dedication, his ferociousness. Vamp slaying ran in his family bloodline and he followed in his dad's footsteps, but to me this battle was new. For years, I never knew there were people who took up the good fight to balance the dark. Dylan introduced me to that side, trained me to defeat the monsters in the shadows.

Then on a routine night he took me out with him, he was killed in action.

Ice wrapped around my heart, and when I closed my eyes, I still saw him ambushed by three vamps as he tried to save me from another. His screams bled in my ears, those huge green eyes flooded with fear, arms reaching for me. He knew that his end had come. It was written all over his terrified face. Then the fuckers took his body with them, maybe as a trophy or to gain favor with a vampire higher up.

I didn't know but I tried to help, charging after

them, but failed miserably. They were gone in the blink of an eye. Ripped him from my life, and I was left to mourn and attend his funeral with no body. Weeks turned into months of sorrow, and I never wanted to experience that agony ever again, to lament the death of anyone close.

My heart was racing, my eyes pricking with tears at the memory that haunted my dreams.

After that night, I picked up the slayer mantle in his place and vowed to fight for him. As it turned out, I had a talent for eliminating vamps. I was stronger than I should have been, and coupled with my ability to sense supernatural and death, well it turned out I was made for this profession.

But Dylan's loss still bled through me at not being able to save him. Just like I couldn't protect my parents.

Nevertheless, somehow since arriving in Anchorage, I'd allowed myself to be overtaken by… what? Plain old curiosity? A starved libido? The allure of forbidden attraction? Or some insidious combination of all of the above? The answer wasn't rocket science. Not all monsters came in hideous packages, and I had given in to a moment of weakness—albeit an extended one.

The rational side of my brain was furious.

These guys weren't just my enemies; they were supposed to be my prey. In a perfect world, I would have neutralized them already and been on my way back to Seattle. Instead, I was fresh out of bed with one of them, and grappling with the shameful knowledge that I wasn't about to say no to either of the others.

What kind of slayer did that make me? If I was employed with the organization of slayers that resided in New York, I could expect to be fired at best, skinned alive at worst. Did this one admittedly monumental indiscretion make me a traitor? Had I just betrayed Dylan's memory?

Those were the thoughts that plagued me as I finally lay down to get some rest in the king-sized bed. I'd have loved to say they kept me up all night, but physical fatigue worked in conjunction with a fortress of extremely fluffy pillows to put me right out. The next time I opened my eyes, it was aggressively bright outside. The sun's rays pried through a gap in the drapes.

I sat up and yawned. My whole body ached with varying degrees of intensity. I could still feel Seth all over me. Ghosts of vague, erotic dreams haunted my recent memory. I shook my head to clear it.

Then the phone on the nightstand next to the bed jangled loudly. I nearly jumped out of my skin.

"Hello?" I had intended to pretend as if I didn't just wake up from ten or eleven hours of much needed sleep, but the thickness in my voice gave me away instantly.

"Sorry to disturb you, miss," said the cheerful voice on the other end of the line. "We're just calling to notify you of a personal delivery waiting for you here in the lobby. You'll need to show ID in order to collect it."

"Uh, okay. I'll be down soon. Thanks." She hung up, and I held the receiver in my hand, looking at it. A delivery from whom? Fifty-fifty chance it was some kind of grisly warning, as historically utilized by the vast majority of organized crime.

Great. Just what I needed, to be on the vamp mafia's certified shit list. I reprimanded myself for my poor life decisions as I threw on some clothes and ran a brush through my hair. All I needed was an ounce of self-control, and I wouldn't be neck deep in this mess. It wasn't until I picked up my cell phone and saw the half dozen texts from Lian that it even crossed my mind the package might be something else entirely.

"Hey, are you up? I can hook you up with a

scanner if you need one," she'd written. Then a couple hours later, "Hello? Figures you'd be sleeping the one time I've got something really useful for you, haha. Call me when you get up!" The most recent one said, "Ugh, never mind. I'm too impatient to wait for you. I'll just send it to the front desk at the Grand, okay? Let me know when you have it!"

My heart jumped in my chest. A police scanner was the one thing my arsenal of skills and tools was missing in Alaska, because of course it was the one thing I hadn't stuffed into my luggage at the last minute. I gargled some mouthwash and ran down to the receptionist, my grogginess forgotten in the face of this new development.

Maybe now I stood a better chance of staying out of trouble. At least for a while.

I had the nondescript box open on my bed inside of six minutes. The model inside was new and fancy, leagues better than the dinosaur sitting on my desk at home. While I fiddled around setting it up, I dictated a text back to Lian.

"Sorry! No sleep finally caught up to me. I crashed out super hard. But love you for this, thank you so much. Let's talk soon?" Right as my phone chimed to let me know the message sent, the speakers on the scanner crackled to life. I grinned. "Now we're talking!"

The mid-afternoon sun poured through the window onto the long desk against that wall as I integrated the scanner into my workstation setup. The audio was crystal clear—the calls might as well have been addressed to me. I wondered if maybe it wasn't worth it to upgrade my equipment after all. Yeah, I loved my trusty old scanner, but this one I could actually hear.

I was ecstatic, so much so, that I called Lian.

Lian answered, "Hey babe, how's the scanner?"

"Insanely amazing. I can't believe you got it for me, but I love you for it."

She giggled over the phone, which made me smile. "Wanted to make sure you had everything you needed to clean up this town."

I could almost see her smile at her sarcasm. Places like Anchorage were so heavily infested with supernaturals, I doubted it was ever possible to eradicate them all. "Well, right now I'm intrigued more and more about the partnership between the clanmaster, Orion and a demon and an angel."

A small gasp come over the phone. "He's the

clanmaster? Shit. Why is he hanging out with a demon and angel?"

"There's a lot more going on here than I first thought, so I need to spend more time studying them. I think I've got one of them on my side who might talk."

She didn't respond at first, then asked in a stern voice, "V, please don't tell me this intrigue is turning into personal interest?"

I scoffed. "As if. You know me well enough. I'm here to stop them." I was worried I didn't know myself that well, seeing I just lied to my friend after she hit the nail on the head.

"Okay, just keep me posted, but I gotta go, someone's calling me. Please stay safe. Bye." She hung up.

I hated the growing unease in my gut that I was letting myself get too close to the enemy on a personal level.

After that, I stepped out of the hotel just long enough to grab some food and snacks, and then I parked my ass right in front of the snazzy new scanner, settling in for a quiet afternoon of eavesdropping on Anchorage's finest. And I had to admit, sitting all cozy in the room beat the hell out of cold, rainy nighttime stakeouts. It was probably a good idea to cool it on those for a while anyway, given that the last one had ended with me literally in bed underneath a demon.

Most of the police calls were pretty standard fare for daytime in a small city. Noise complaints, public disturbances, traffic stops, the usual. I spent a little time familiarizing myself with the local codes, and then comfortably let the stream of calls drone on in the background while I organized my notes. As the afternoon moved on toward evening, the reports became a little more serious. Breaking-and-entering, a few thefts, an assault following a fight at a gas station downtown.

"Dispatch to all units in the downtown area, we've got an 11-1 called in just now. All available units, please respond. 11-1, all units please respond."

I snapped to attention, my pen freezing above the page. Dispatch rattled off an address not too far from the Grand Hotel. 11-1 was the Anchorage PD's code for homicide. In progress or not, I wasn't able to tell. As I sat stock still at the desk, waiting for details, all other sound in the world drained away. My senses focused on the words coming out of the scanner.

Within seconds, the airwaves were briefly

choked by squad cars calling in their responses. I held my breath, fingers clenched tightly around the pen. One mention of a strange-looking corpse and I'd be on my way. Gray skin, no blood, neck wound—didn't matter what it was. Every muscle in my body was primed and ready.

But clarification didn't come easily, even after the first cops arrived on the scene. The first thing they did was start to report discovery of bodies. More than one. By the time the officer had counted to four, I was up and grabbing my hunter's belt. They were already far out of their depth. Fortunately, it wouldn't take long to get there.

The sun hovered just above the horizon as I left the hotel, sitting low in a blood-red sky. I was never a big believer in mystical omens, but it was hard not to take it as an ominous sign of things to come. I wondered what I would find on scene, and whether or not the police had managed to cordon things off already. I picked up my pace; if I moved fast, I might be able to beat them to investigating the scene.

The road leading up to the crime scene headed right into the woods, and it was in the process of being blocked off. A line of police cars formed a temporary barricade, their lights casting the dirty snow and darkening day in intermittent reds and blues. On the approach, I saw an officer with a huge roll of yellow tape starting to establish a perimeter, and I thought better of advancing. No way would a supposed citizen be allowed anywhere near multiple fatalities. The more I peered around, the curved street and houses revealed nothing. That told me the incident happened perhaps at the end of the street, closer to woods... or perhaps just beyond the edge of the forest.

But maybe I could trick a little extra information out of them. The best investigators were extremely tight-lipped, but they were also not usually the first ones on site. I wove a long path around until it looked like I was coming from the other side of the road, heading toward the hotel. Twenty yards from the police barricade, I stopped and looked confused. An officer came up to me, waving his hand.

"Sorry, miss. You can't come through here. Road's closed."

I blinked innocently. "But I just came through here a couple hours ago and everything was fine."

He scrutinized me. "It's a recent development,

and I'm afraid it's very serious. Where are you trying to go?"

I frowned. "I'm staying at the hotel over there. Are you sure you can't just let me under the tape real quick?" These were abhorrent, annoying questions to ask any law enforcement officer in the middle of securing a violent scene, but I wanted to know if he'd let anything slip.

He shook his head. "I'm sorry, ma'am. A crime has been committed. I can't let you across this line." Still wanting to help, he turned in the direction of the Grand Hotel and pointed out a detour. "If you cross here and head that way a few blocks, it'll take you down near where you want to be."

I sighed. "Okay. Thank you, sir."

A voice came across the cop's radio and summoned him away, which was perfect timing. The moment his back was turned, I got the hell out of there. The beginnings of a crowd of rubber-neckers was forming outside the tape. I disappeared among them, transitioning from the small sea of interested faces into the protection of the trees that surrounded this town. I'd go the long way around to reach the scene. The going was a little tough, as well as being wet, slushy, and icy in the woodland, but I picked my way along parallel to the scene. With any luck, there'd be an adjoining clearing or some other space I might use as a vantage point to an unobstructed view.

Every ten seconds or so, I shut my eyes and let my senses lead me toward the epicenter of the incident. I had known from minute one that vamps were not likely to be involved, based on time of day alone. But I also knew at that point that ruling out vampires didn't exactly narrow down my options. Anchorage had become a teeming petri dish of supernatural energy, ever shifting, ever evolving.

There was no way to tell what I'd encounter, so I was loaded for anything at all. The closer I got, the more confusing my intuition became. The prime energy signature was nothing I had ever seen before, and it was splashed all over. I could practically see it in my mind's eye, like blood detected under Luminol at crime scenes. The auras of its victims were shattered like glass, spread in a huge radius around the bodies. I know for certain these victims I sensed were humans…innocents. None of them were supernaturals, which told me two things.

First, the attacks weren't a result of the vampire clan fights.

Second, I was certain something else was hunting humans in Anchorage.

"What the fuck happened here?" I whispered. "What could do this?"

In my pocket, my phone vibrated. I ducked behind a tree to check it, just in case.

"I thought you'd never answer," Lian said. "Whenever works for you."

"Give me a rain check," I told her. "Something came up."

And then, at the same moment that I tucked my phone away again, I became abruptly aware of a presence nearby—a living one.

I had company.

I followed Veronica at a distance, the falling night concealing me as I puzzled over her actions. As a slayer in close contact with any number of supernaturals, including us, why was she speaking to the police? She knew firsthand that Orion's relationship with law enforcement couldn't be great—not if he was disposing of victims off the bank of an icy river. It seemed like an unnecessary flirtation with trouble to be interacting with the officers at all.

But they didn't think of detaining her, and she managed to slip away unnoticed by anyone other than me. I tracked her deep into the trees, closer and closer to the imprint of death that stained the atmosphere. Could she feel that heavy shroud? I sensed the unusual energy from her back in Orion's house. There was something very different about her, but I couldn't pinpoint it. Which was strange in itself.

If she had any misgivings, they weren't reflected in her smooth, confident stride. She appeared to be a woman on a mission.

I didn't have to speculate about how grisly the scene would be. I could smell the thick, metallic stench of blood on the cold breeze. Currents of violent energy whipped around me, strong enough to rival Seth's demonic rage. At first, I thought it could have been him visiting destruction on whoever happened to cross his path. It wouldn't have been the first time a random stranger bore the brunt of his fury.

This time, however, the aura that remained was foreign to me. I paused for a minute to try and identify its distinctive signature, without success. When I looked up to resume tailing Veronica, she was gone. Softly, I cursed myself for looking away in the first place. She might have been mortal, but she was crafty. She knew better than most how to disappear.

I stepped forward along the same trajectory she'd been traveling, all senses open. Unless she had used some type of magic, she couldn't have gotten far. Sure enough, in a matter of yards, I saw her pop back out in front of me. Then she stopped in her tracks and glanced around.

I'd gotten too close. The game was up. Veronica turned.

"Logan?" Her tone registered more surprise than anything; maybe I'd caught her more off guard than I thought. She stared at me with bald curiosity. "What are you doing here?"

"I could ask you the same," I replied. "Do you know where you're going?" What I really wanted to say was, *Do you know what you're about to see?* Intuition told me it wasn't going to be pretty.

"Sort of." She shrugged. "Something tells me it won't exactly be hard to miss." Her gaze sharpened and turned searching. "You know something about this, don't you?" Immediately, all of her walls went up. I saw her body tense, flight or fight response kicking into gear. It was funny, in a way, that she was so prepared to fight me. As if she stood a chance.

"Not as much as you think I do." I held up my hand, moving forward so that we were almost standing beside one another. "Relax. Let's go."

Veronica hesitated initially. She didn't want to

fall into step with me, which was fine. Once she saw me proceeding forward without her, she changed her mind very quickly. "Wait. Is this you helping me?"

I laughed. "No. This is me not hurting you." If she thought I was going to void my bargain with Orion for her sake, she was quite wrong. But I had never been a strong advocate of baseless cruelty. She could, as far as I was concerned, do whatever she wanted. Provided that she stayed out of my way.

She walked beside me in complicated silence for half a minute before speaking up again. "I don't understand you, Logan."

"I am sure that's true," I agreed. "Our kind is rare."

She twisted a bright lock of hair around her finger. "Forgive me if this is an insensitive thing to ask, but how is it that you become…what you are?"

When was the last time someone—anyone— had asked me for forgiveness? Against my better judgment, I felt myself warming to her. "What do you know about angels?" The question was sincere, and slightly playful.

She smiled a little. "I admit there is a lot I don't know. Even the ones who are, um…pre-fall."

I carried with me the spirit of exile, a lonely shadow. The mark of no true belonging.

"I'm sorry," she said. "Don't talk about it if you don't want to. I'm just interested."

I cast her a sidelong glance. She kept her gaze fixed directly ahead, avoiding mine. The apples of her cheeks glowed with the hint of a blush. In my very soul, I knew I could be removed for following in Seth's footsteps with regard to Veronica. There was no need at all to make my own life immeasurably more difficult.

Yet the creeping tendrils of temptation threatened to take root. Had we not been steps from the edge of a murder scene, I might have been in trouble. But the trees were beginning to thin out in the preamble to a small clearing that backed onto a residential street. My mind's eye showed me the dead in various states of repose. Their blood coated the surrounding vegetation in dark, rusty splashes.

"Here," I said to Veronica, our previous conversation all but forgotten. It was a word of warning.

She stopped and sucked in her breath, locking the air into her lungs for a long time. When she finally exhaled, it was with a single word. "Wow."

The far side of the clearing crawled with

uniformed officers. A series of searingly bright flashbulbs detonated in the night, illuminating the carnage strewn across the frosted ground. The light reflected off of dull, dead eyes, splayed hands and fingers, wounds ripped into torsos. Some of the men were more stoic than I might have anticipated—others, not so much. One patrolman staggered off into the opposite line of woods. I saw him bend over with his hands on his knees, retching.

"Is it what you expected?" I asked Veronica softly, leaning in closer to her.

"I don't know." Her voice was flat, drained of nuance. "What happened?" Once more, she pivoted toward me. "I don't believe you're totally clueless about this, Logan. And honestly, I'm not going to push you on your reasons, because I am telling the truth when I say I'm only here to help. Okay? So it would be incredibly generous of you to clue me in on what you do know." Her eyes were earnest and imploring. "Maybe I can help you, too. With whatever it is you're trying to accomplish."

I smiled at her, tucking that stray lock of hair behind her ear. "I wouldn't say that if I were you."

Veronica rolled her eyes. "I take back some of what I said before. You do have some common ground with the other two; you're all *dramatic.*" Her gaze shifted from me back to the activity in the clearing, impatiently surveying our surroundings. "I wish there was a way to get closer."

Her resolve impressed me. Other than a fleeting moment of shock and awe, this woman had displayed no reluctance to investigate, no fear. If anything, she seemed annoyed by the continuing presence of the police. That surprised me.

"That would be difficult at present. I suspect they'd have questions for you."

"I know." She pressed her lips together. "Damn it. I should have waited. I don't even know what I'll be able to find over there. Maybe this one is out of my depth." The frustration was written largely on her pretty face. She folded her arms over her chest and huffed quietly.

I'm not sure what made me do it, but I was suddenly possessed by an almost visceral urge to aid her. She was straining to reach beyond her boundaries and into uncharted territory. Was that what I admired about her? Or was it the full curve of her lips, the tantalizing hollow between her neck and her collarbone, the way her long, dark eyelashes dusted her cheeks when she blinked?

Perhaps I'd never know. And perhaps it didn't

matter. The next thing I knew, I heard my voice offering to join our efforts.

"It's possible I could be of some assistance." I spoke casually, as if this whole exchange meant little in my eyes. "With your permission, that is."

"You *are* helping me." A little smirk tugged at the corner of her mouth. I wanted to be insulted, but the outrage refused to manifest. "Fine, I'll bite. What have you got?"

"You'll find out." I may have plunged into the deep end, but I wasn't about to give every secret away. "Tell me when you want to meet again."

"Here?" She raised an eyebrow.

"Where else?"

"Right." She glanced at the whirlwind of officers marching on and off the scene, their boots leaving a mess of prints in the snow. "Well, I don't see them finding much of anything here. Nothing they can use, anyway. Why don't we give it forty-eight hours, and then we can come back and scope things out again?"

I nodded. "Sounds reasonable."

She regarded me closely. "Promise you're not going to ditch and make me look like an idiot for trusting you. Because that's what I'm doing right now, Logan. I'm trusting you."

As if I could parse her motivations any better. "Forty-eight hours," I said. "I'll be here. That will have to be good enough."

Veronica held out her hand. "All right. Shake on it, then, and let's get the hell out of here before they see us."

We shook hands. On the way back out, I let her go ahead of me, and then I veered off her path, looping through the forest.

If she stopped, or if she looked for me, I didn't see her, nor would she see me. And that was exactly how I wanted it to be.

Whether or not she thought I was ancient, Veronica had forced me to realize how much of my life had gotten stale. Seeing her was like taking a shot of adrenaline directly into a vein. It was a small relief to know that her liaison with Seth had not diminished my desire for her. If anything, my passion soared to new heights, fueled by seething jealousy. Coupled with that, her words about her not being necessarily just exclusive with me played on my mind a lot. I still hadn't worked out how to overcome the jealousy inside me, but the thought percolated.

In turn, I began to brainstorm ways in which I might successfully turn her. Before she came into my sphere of awareness, I would've considered the very notion unconscionable. Veronica was far from the first enticing, attractive young woman I had sired into a vampire, but it had been decades since the last attempt.

And there were several good reasons for that. Whenever those memories threatened to creep to the surface of my consciousness, I shoved them down deep. She would be different. She had to be.

*And what if your precious, beautiful Veronica goes rogue, like the others? What if you have to put her down?*

The possibility, however remote, was agonizing. Part of me wanted so much to push her away and save us both from the suffering that often seemed inevitable. But another, larger part figured that if we were going to be dragged into an eternal hell, we might as well go together.

It was too late for anything else, really. I already thought of Veronica as mine.

The sound of the house phone ringing was so foreign to my ears that it barely registered. I doubted anyone has called us on it since we moved in here. Annoyed, I grabbed it blindly off the cradle on the table where he sat, prepared to either ignore the call or deliver a blistering criticism.

I answered the phone, "Hello."

"It's me," she said. Veronica's voice was low and furtive, as if she thought the line might be tapped. "Got a minute?"

The moment I heard her voice, my entire perspective shifted. "Maybe." The answer was yes, but I wasn't about to give her the satisfaction of knowing it. "What for? And how did you get our number?" I didn't even know the number.

"It's very easy to track down house phone numbers if you know where to search on the web. Anyway, there was an incident earlier tonight. Like an hour ago. I couldn't get too close, but there were a bunch of people dead, from what I saw. And…Logan showed up."

"Oh?" I leaned forward. "Now you have my attention. Are you sure it was him?"

"Couldn't misidentify him if I tried," she answered. "We talked face to face."

Automatically, my fist clenched in my lap. A hot flare of temper flushed my vision red. How could it be that both of the henchmen I had so judiciously hired were spending more time with my prize than I was? "And what did he want to discuss?"

"Not much. I was hoping you'd be able to give

me a little more insight on him." She paused. "That is, if it's convenient for you."

I hesitated, considering. The possibility of a trap was not lost on me. I suspected Veronica was as skilled as she was gorgeous, and she'd already shown her nerves of steel. It took a lot of guts to come waltzing into a vamp territory as tightly knit as Anchorage. She may have decided to turn some of that admirable boldness against me.

"There must be some give and take involved. Surely you understand my unwillingness to take a blind risk without compensation." There. The line had been drawn. I sat back and waited for her return fire.

"I thought you might say that," she responded without missing a beat. "Come to my room at the Grand Hotel. We can work something out."

I didn't need much more convincing. "I'll hold you to that, Veronica." If she tried to back out after I got there, I was fully prepared to negotiate by any means necessary.

"Of course you will," she answered. "See you soon."

I was still on high alert, as always, but not going to seek out trouble. With any luck, there would be no violence tonight. I could only hope Veronica felt the same. I set the phone down and headed out. It was strange but refreshing to be walking in downtown Anchorage without an ulterior motive.

The lobby of the Grand Hotel was empty at that hour, and I bypassed it entirely. Veronica's energy shone like a beacon, as easy to follow as if the way had been marked with signs. I tracked her up to the fifth floor—room 502—and knocked gently. She made me wait approximately fifteen seconds.

"Well, look who's here." Veronica leaned in the doorway, eyeing me through her long lashes. Her pink hair had been swept over one shoulder as though she'd been playing with it. She wore casual blue jeans, tight mesh top over a white sleeveless top with thin straps. And white socks, adding to that casual but sexy vixen look. "I have to admit, I kind of thought you wouldn't show."

"And miss an opportunity to spend time with you?" I smirked. "Perish the thought." She stepped back from the threshold and started to turn around. I stopped her. "Veronica."

"What?" She looked at me quizzically.

"You're forgetting something." I glanced at the floor and back at her.

"Am I?" She smiled slightly.

I sighed. Okay, so maybe she had some traditions to learn. But she was smart, and I had no doubt she'd be able to keep up. "You need to invite me inside."

"Ohhh." Veronica looked me up and down. She chuckled, putting a slender hand to her mouth. "I'm sorry. I didn't know that was a real thing."

I furrowed my brow. "You've been a slayer for how long without knowing that?"

She rolled her pale blue eyes. "Sue me if I don't typically invite my enemies into my house." Tossing her hair, she waved me on. "Here. Would you like to come inside?"

"Thank you," I said wryly. She led me down the short hall into the main common area of her suite. Positioned against the wall underneath the window, a desk sat piled high with papers, photographs, files, and a very new police scanner.

"Don't look over there," Veronica urged as soon as she caught me. "Just because we're in talks doesn't mean the treaty's been signed."

"Noted." I sat down in one of the two armchairs that afforded the best view of her. She stayed on her feet. "Now, let's talk. You want to know about Logan."

"Do you think he's a double agent?" Veronica pulled no punches with her line of questioning.

"Of course not," I scoffed. "I have foolproof ways of ensuring his allegiance. He wouldn't dare try anything…unwise." It was a scenario I'd wondered about on my own, more times than I wanted to admit. To me, Seth read like an open book, all his volatile moods on full display. Logan was closely guarded, brimming with more secrets than I was able to ferret out of him.

I never truly knew what he was thinking, a reality I found deeply unsettling.

"Then what would you guess he was doing there?" she pressed. "Just happened to be in the neighborhood?"

"Hold on a moment." I stared at her sternly. "Before I consent to any more of this interrogation, I was told there was a bargain to be made." My gaze raked over her immaculate form. I licked my lips. "What do you have to say about that?"

Veronica's eyes bored into mine, full of intensity and yearning. "I am prepared to make a fair trade." Her lips lingered on the word "fair."

I reached out, stroking the side of her clothed thigh with my palm. Her jeans felt like a second skin under my touch. She was so warm and alive.

My hunger rose like the tide. I could no longer help myself. My fingers tightened around the back of her leg, just below her right buttock. Veronica gave a tiny gasp.

"Stop me if this isn't what you want," I told her bluntly.

She didn't.

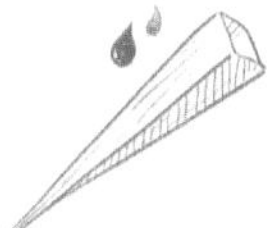

It would probably have killed Orion to know that the first thing I thought of when he touched me was Seth, but I couldn't control raw thought association. Nor could I help making the comparison—Orion's smooth, deep-running power versus the force and excitement of the demon. When Orion drew me close as he sat in the chair, there was none of the wild heat that constantly emanated off of Seth's person. But still, an electric thrill shot up my spine.

I didn't even think about stopping him. His right hand moved to grip my ass, the other arm snaking its way around my waist. In one swift motion, Orion pulled me down into his lap. We were inches apart, our faces almost touching. My hands came to rest on his chest.

"You don't have a heartbeat," I observed, like the smartest person in the world. Never would have thought a vampire had the ability to get me flustered, but there we were. I made a plan to do what was needed to get insider information, but deep in my mind I was also secretly excited about exploring the unusual attraction I held for my enemy. I slayed vampires, not slept with them. Yet, I was prepared to make an exception for the sake of gaining intelligence. I almost laughed at myself at how transparent I'd become. He'd been on my mind since first crossing paths with him and left me lusting over him, so this was me getting him out of my system once and for all, I kept telling myself.

"Does that bother you?" He caressed my cheek with the back of one cool hand.

"Not as much as it should," I admitted.

His hand flipped to cup my face, and then our lips met. They were cold to the touch. He kissed me slowly at first, but then the gates of passion crashed wide open. I moaned as he slipped his tongue into my mouth. My legs wrapped around him, straddling him, pressed tightly to him.

"I should have guessed you'd be so eager to get in bed with your adversaries," Orion murmured. The points of his teeth grazed my neck just enough that I felt them on my skin. "How far are you willing to go?"

"Don't push your luck," I warned.

He grinned and pulled my top over my head. I shook my hair out of my face and went for his buttons, my fingers clumsy with excitement. I ran my palms over his strong planes of muscles... everything about this vampire was deliriously gorgeous. The way he stared at me made me feel confident, stunning, and sexy as hell. I met his gaze, and there was something I didn't expect behind his those spectacular eyes. Tenderness. I thought his main reason for accepting would come down to pure lust. I'd seen the way he studied me before, but I didn't anticipate something this soft in the clanmaster's gaze.

If someone had told me I'd be getting it on with both a demon and a vampire within a week, I wouldn't have believed them for a second. And yet, he was taking my bra off, running his long tongue along the curve of my breast.

I trembled with desire in response, breathing heavily, my panties soaking wet.

I couldn't believe how badly I wanted him. When he lifted me deftly into his arms and carried me to the bed, I let him. I even let him toss me down onto the mattress. He ran his hands over my whole upper body, tracing the contours of my waist, kissing the tip of each nipple. Then he pushed down my pants. He yanked them off before tossing them behind him. He unbuttoned his own pants and dropped them, kicking them aside.

My gaze settled on his erection, so hard and thick, the tip coated in pre-cum. Elation swept through me at the promise of what was coming for me. My core ached for his touch, for this vampire to show me what he had planned for me. The thought left me quivering, but I couldn't forget that at the end of the day, he was still a monster.

An incredibly handsome monster, but still deadly.

"Let me be clear about one thing, Orion," I said between deep, hungry kisses. "If I feel so much as the ghost of one of your eyeteeth anywhere near my jugular, I'm shutting the whole thing down. And then I will kick your ass into next fucking year before you even get your clothes back on."

Orion pushed his mouth down against mine,

growling into my lips, "I love it when you talk dirty."

He was a dominant lover, even more so than Seth had been. It was obvious that he got a real kick out of dictating my pleasure. Without hesitation, he pushed open my bent legs, lowering his gaze and himself onto the bed. I caught the smirk curling on his mouth, sending delicious tingles down my spine. His mouth sealed over my heat, and I arched with pleasure. The strange sensation of something cold against my fiery offering turned me on ridiculously. He teased my clit with the tip of his tongue until I gasped and trembled, my hands balled into fists around the sheets. Desperate, I braced my feet on the bedspread and pushed up against his tongue, throwing back my head in anticipation of ecstasy.

"Give it to me," I moaned.

He drew a tantalizing circle around my clit. "Tell me you want it, Veronica."

"You son of a bitch." I glared at him, panting. "This isn't fair." But he wouldn't budge, so I relented. "I want it so bad. Please."

"That's a good girl." I felt him smile as he sucked me hard, slipping his fingers inside me at the same time. My body writhed on its own. I grabbed his wrist with both my hands. I think I howled.

What happened after that, took place in a red haze of primal desire. He made his way up my body, leaving a trail of kisses and licks around my budding nipples, taking one into his mouth, sucking hard, then bestowing the same attention to the other. Sweeping his mouth over my collarbone and neck, I stiffened at him lingering just below my earlobe. I sensed him tensing as his hardness teased my entrance. He caged me in with his arms on either side of my shoulders, and I bucked up against him, but he refused to give me what I wanted. After I had come to the point of rigid shaking, I flipped him over without any pause. He grunted, surprised, but didn't fight back. I shuffled down his body and maintained eye contact as I took his cock in my hand and slipped my mouth over it. Orion clenched his jaw, breath hissing between his teeth.

"You're perfect," he whispered.

As payment for the compliment, I worked him over hard, exploring his shaft and balls with my tongue, moaning as I licked and sucked him. He tasted salty and sweet at the same time. It wasn't long before he was throbbing, his eyes blazing with lust. Instead of allowing me to finish him off with my mouth, he pulled me up to straddle him. I lifted my hips and let him guide them back down onto his waiting cock.

I gnawed on my lower lip as he slid into me, stretching me wider, and I loved every fucking ache.

"I want to watch you," he mused.

I gasped as he pushed deeper into me, and I shifted to spread myself wider to accommodate his size. Pushing myself to sit upright on him, I took a deep breath, settling over his hardness, letting him fully fill me.

"You are stunning."

Then I rode him as hard as my body would allow, bouncing up and down on him, his eyes searing over my jiggling breasts. The whole world melted away for a few minutes, leaving only our bodies gyrating together, the sensation of him filling me with every thrust. Every so often, he'd pull me up higher, maximizing his depth. In those moments, he often hit a spot deep inside that made me see stars.

"Shit," I moaned. "Shit!" Frantic and on the edge, I leaned forward over him, grasping the headboard in both hands. I floated on the edge of ecstasy, desperate for that release.

As if sensing my need, Orion grasped my hips, fingers digging into flesh as he hissed his arousal.

With his help, my hips worked in a frenzy on top of him until I finally went sailing over the crest of that wave. It crashed into me so fast, it consumed me whole. The sounds I made were guttural, pulled from my chest. As long as he was in me, I could not stop coming.

Orion tangled a hand in my hair and pulled my head back, kissing my throat and chest. He growled against my lips, his body tensing, and he pulsed inside me. We were one, locked together and the moment was so perfect.

I gasped. Every inch of my body trembled. My legs were weak, and I didn't remember how long I rode him when I finally came down from the clouds. I moaned gently as I slowed down.

When he disentangled us at last, I sort of collapsed in the bed beside him on my stomach. "Holy fuck."

Orion stretched out beside me like the god he was. His fingers, blessedly cool, traced a delicate pattern along my spine. He wasn't flushed like I was, but I noticed with some gratification that he was sweating somehow. He had a look on his face that reminded me of a contented predator toying with his prey.

"You are unlike anyone else I've ever been with." His fingers never stopped stroking down my back, luring me into a relaxed state. "I think that will do for now," he said, his voice colored by a hint of smugness. "I must say, I'm blown away with your performance, darling. It's an image that will never leave me."

"Mm-hmm." I was so worn out, half drunk on endorphins, that all the questions I still wanted to ask simply leaked from my brain. I let my face sink into the pillow. My eyelids wanted to drop closed and stay that way indefinitely. "Thanks."

He leaned over and kissed the crown of my head. "Sweet dreams, Veronica. We'll talk about the angel some other time."

"Wait." I shook my head, making a vain attempt to rouse myself. "No, we should discuss him now. That was part of the deal."

In response, Orion kissed me once more. He eased me back down and massaged my scalp with his fingertips until I was back to teetering on the edge of oblivion. "Don't worry about it for now," he murmured. "I'm a man of my word. I won't forget."

That was the last thing I heard before sleep claimed me.

Upon waking, I found the bed beside me empty. No sign of the vampire clanmaster remained, other than the sexy musky smell of him in the sheets and the sweet ache between my legs.

"Ah, damn it." I rolled onto my back and stared at the dark ceiling, hugging a pillow to my chest. I cursed myself for proposing such a deal in the first place. I knew the answer, though. His presence had unleashed something inside me, and I stupidly let myself follow my lust instead of my head. I'd let myself fall for a vampire and demon, and now they were both engraved on my thoughts. They were enemies, yet I craved them madly.

"What the hell am I doing?"

There was no answer, except for the faint whine of an eerie Alaskan wind on the other side of the window.

I couldn't tell exactly when it had happened, but at some point in the very recent past, my feelings about our little three-person enterprise had begun to change. Specifically, I wasn't sure if Orion's silver-tongued promises were worth the suffering anymore. To bite my tongue and hold my fists in the face of endless harassment from outsiders was bitter agony for me.

With every passing minute, the urge to unleash this pent-up anger mounted dangerously. It boiled just below the surface of my outward veneer of calm. At any moment, I felt I could snap and transform into the monster I wanted to be. The one with the freedom to rampage until I was spent and could be calm again.

It wasn't often that my fights with Orion left me sour. Usually, one destructive outburst was all I needed to set me back on an even keel for a while. But this time, I wasn't so lucky. Instead of being relieved, I cultivated resentment. Who was he, a dead man, a walking corpse, to tell me what I could and couldn't do?

Besides, the girl had clearly enjoyed herself. My mouth watered just thinking about her. Man, she was delicious. There was something to be said about forbidden fruits—they always turned out to be the sweetest. But then, why was Orion the one who got to determine what was and wasn't forbidden? I shoved my hands into my pockets and glowered heavily as I marched down the hall of our house. I needed air.

Orion stepped out of the living room as I walked past. I should have just kept going, but instead I stopped. Veronica refused to leave my mind, along with Orion's insistence she was his, and it would burn me up if I remained silent. "Listen, I don't normally care what you do with your personal life and all that shit, but when it comes to Veronica—"

"She's open to several men in her life," he interrupted me.

I flinched, taken aback by his comment. "Say again? She said this to you, and you're okay with sharing?"

Orion snorted. "That wasn't what I said. But before you got all ballistic, I wanted you to know her opinion."

I eyed him as he stood there, hands deep in the pockets of his black pants, and I searched his face for the truth. "It must have killed you to hear her say that."

"I always get what I want, Seth. But I'm not a fucking monster and am open minded." Tightness crowded around the corners of his lips. "Thought you should know and maybe we can try to mend whatever's the hell's going on between us."

Again, I wasn't sure where his sudden caring nature came from. Maybe guilt, or maybe in realizing that if he wanted Veronica, he might have to concede to what she wanted. For once I was lost for words.

Part of me respected Orion more in that moment more than I had in forever. Though, I fought the urge to burst out laughing to see the grand vampire leader showing a softer side because of a mortal. That was fascinating.

"Is that all?" I asked, struck by a strange awkwardness between us.

He nodded and turned down the hallway, putting distance between us.

Outside, I couldn't come to terms with what Orion just dropped on me. I cruised along the sidewalk, going over it again and again.

I get he had been pissed that I claimed her first. The bastard didn't want my sloppy seconds. I grinned wickedly at that. Except, V's reveal stunned me as much as it clearly had Orion.

"Hey!" The shout jerked me out of my funk, and I came to a stop on the sidewalk, looking around like I'd just snapped out of hypnosis. "Watch where you're fucking going, asshole!"

"Who are you calling an asshole?!"

The voices filtered back to me from their origin point at the end of an alley up ahead. I turned toward them out of a mix of curiosity and a need for distraction. The closer I got, the more voices I heard, until the words had devolved into a jumble of thickly layered interactions. Most of them were shouting, words ringing through the air like stray bullets from a gun.

"What don't you get about this, man?" A young man stood blocking the mouth of the alley, poised in a fighting stance. "We don't want you city rats around here anymore. Consider your welcome overstayed." The last sentence was punctuated by cheers, clapping, a lone shrill whistle. His boys pulled in tight around him.

A fight was brewing. I craned my neck, peering through the blackness to try and get a look at the other side. They were bunched up at the alley's dead end. Disadvantaged, maybe, but nothing close to defeated. I had seen the looks on their faces before from cornered animals making a desperate bid for freedom.

"And what don't *you* get, assclown? We're not going anywhere anytime soon!" The vamp on the far end had no discernible accent, but he moved with the practiced aggression of a city dweller, a man who made a habit of squaring off with rival gangs at least once a night. He was a foreigner, an out-of-towner. One of Orion's enemies from the Seattle clan, I guessed.

I should have called him right then. Except these pricks had pushed me far enough. Rather than calming down and walking away from a situation that had very little to do with me, I stepped forward, shoving through the small crowd.

"How about this?" I raised my voice so it would carry. "You're all douchebags and this ain't nothing more than a mediocre circle-jerk. Can we agree on that?"

They all turned and looked at me, their eyes glowing dully. The resulting effect was eerie enough to raise goosebumps on my skin, which I promptly shook off. "Get the fuck out of here," I ordered. "All of you. Now."

They looked at each other. "Says you and what army?" the first vamp demanded snidely. "We were here first. If anyone should be getting lost, it's you."

"Butt out, will you?" the Seattle vamp added. "Things are complicated enough without your ugly ass trying to interfere. Go back to the circus or whatever hole you crawled out of, you freak."

"Nah." I advanced into the alleyway, spreading my arms in the universal challenge-issuing gesture. "I'd rather we settle this here and now, wouldn't you?" The faster I plummeted headlong toward a bad decision, the less bad it seemed. My knuckles burned with unused heat. I wanted to brand one of these wise guys right across the cheek.

The vamps exchanged looks. A murmur swept through their ranks. If I had been paying even slightly closer attention, I might have picked up on some clues that would've helped me avert the crisis that was seconds from occurring. But of course I missed every sign. I was too wrapped up in imagining the glory of fighting.

"C'mon, boys and girls." The Seattle vamp cracked his neck. "Let's show him what we've got." With a sweeping motion of his arm, he led the charge straight down the center of the alley. I braced myself and met him with my shoulder. He reeled back, dazed. His nose looked off center after the collision. I felt a little bad about it, but not enough to reevaluate my attack strategy.

Good thing, too. They came in from all sides, swarming like a horde of insects. I didn't get a chance to see where every one of them came from, nor how they kept arriving. The first couple waves were bearable, almost routine. I threw all kinds of vamps in all kinds of directions, sending them sprawling and scattering. Massive tongues of flame singed the brick walls on either side.

Then, as the numbers refused to diminish, I realized I might have a problem. There was no stemming the endless tide of the undead fuckers.

And they were relentless, jumping right back after I'd brush them off. It took a long time, but I started to get tired. My punches turned sluggish. I didn't want to move.

How could there be so many?

I fought as long as I was physically able, but in the end, they managed to restrain me. The hard ground underneath my face was almost a relief. I didn't even care that they seemed to be celebrating my downfall.

"What should we do with him?" A circle of vampiric faces crowded around me. It was interesting to note that the crowd had chosen at some point to desegregate. Alaskan and Seattle vamps glared at me in unison.

"Throw him to the cops," one said gruffly. "Tell them he's the one behind that killing a mile from here. It doesn't matter if he's not. They're looking for someone to blame, and it'll get them off our backs."

"Hmm. That's not a bad idea." A dozen heads gazed down at me. I felt like some dead stiff right before the autopsy.

"Screw off," I muttered, somewhat less impressively than I meant it. It was dawning on me, slowly and unpleasantly, that I had been drained from the fight. I could barely lift my arms. The side of my face melted into the floor.

"Will he die if we leave him?" someone asked. It would've been touching if not for the hard edge of practicality around every syllable.

"If he does, he's no good as a patsy," came the reply. The vamps concurred, and a few of the strongest stepped forward. They grabbed me around the armpits and dragged me to my feet. "Don't make trouble," they warned. One of them tied a blindfold around my eyes. "And don't peek. This is classified information."

That was how I ended up in the back of a moving vampire caravan, being packed off to some secret hideaway in Anchorage. I sat staring at the jet black dark on the inside of the blindfold, cursing my own conceit. It would've been so easy just to keep my big mouth shut. As a last act of defiance, I rattled my restraints.

"Shut it," snapped a vamp. "Just sit there and look ugly, will you?"

I wanted to kill him. But exhaustion made my body seem like it was filled with sand. For the moment, all I could do was obey.

That alone damn near killed me.

# CHAPTER 25

## VERONICA

The next forty-eight hours passed at an agonizing crawl. I couldn't focus on anything other than the three men who had suddenly swept in and taken over so much of my world. Orion had not been in contact since the visit he had paid me at the hotel, and I knew when not to push an issue. Besides, much like my tryst with Seth, I still wasn't sure how I felt about it. That wasn't what I came to Anchorage for, yet I found myself tangled with them. My mission was always to observe, learn what was going on first, then jump into battle. But that was seeming less possible with each passing day.

But standing around in my hotel room was driving me crazy, and the police scanner offered no insight into anything potentially supernatural, so I got dressed, added my stake, extendable staff, and blade to my belt, then covered it with my thick jacket. Stepping into my boots, I made the call that my watching time was over. I needed to get involved and end the battle that would eventually spill into killing innocents if not stopped.

Dressed warmly, I went into my bag of weapons.

I slid the blade on the sheath on my belt, a stake, both of which I carried backups. Then I grabbed my extendable silver cylinder and hung it off my pocket which worked best as a long stake.

An icy wind greeted me at the sliding doors of the hotel. Chin tugged low, I folded my hands over my stomach and rushed out to the sidewalk. Fresh snow crunched underfoot, and I hurried onward.

Over the day and a half that followed, I spent a lot of time shaking my head and wrestling with complicated emotions. The problems I faced in the moment could not have looked more different than the ones I left behind in Seattle. Who had time to worry about schoolwork and rescheduling exams? I was caught in the quagmire of a potential love rectangle, between lovers who lived together even as they struggled to tolerate each other.

My head spun with the feelings that searing feeling inside I held for the three men. Three enemies... and whatever was going on between us was different. I'd never felt this way before. Other slayers had fallen prey to the allure of vampires, and I'd seen it personally myself. I never understood the attraction, the dynamics... until now. Well, in truth, I still didn't understand how I could be so drawn to them when I had one mission. Find and stop the vampire killings. I'd done the first part and found the killings, but the second part was a lot more complicated. There was a clan war going on, and if Orion was wiped out, was the next monster to step into his shoes going to start butchering humans more openly? Orion's followers didn't seem to practice this or there would be more innocents killed.

Then my thoughts swung to the gruesome scene from earlier... who was responsible for that?

I had more questions than answers to understand what was going on here. There was something I still remembered Dylan would say to me often. He'd compare vampire actions to the ice berg principle. The attacks they carry out were only ten percent of the real story that explained their behavior. It was so much more than feeding, he had said. But I wasn't sure I believed him. The assholes who killed my parents seemed to be there for the purpose of feeding. Not to mention the two in the alleyway attacking the young boy shortly after I arrived in Anchorage.

Dylan taught me a lot of new things, and I followed his approach as I only got into slaying after he passed, after watching him kill the wicked, after I needed to do something to put out the inferno burning me up from the inside out. That came in the form of eliminating vamps.

I shook away those thoughts because it felt like I was going in circles. There was so much I needed to uncover. Plus, would it really hurt if I scoured the streets and took out any fiends who got in my way?

Bright lights lit up the dark street. People strolled from one store to the next quickly, carrying grocery bags, or heading into the local bar. Normal life, but how did they feel about living so close to the supernatural? Most didn't know about them, or turned a blind eye to anything strange happening. But in a place like this, how could they really not see how many creatures lived right under their noses.

The thought brought me to Orion, Seth, and

Logan. How exactly had the trio found each other? They were an odd bunch, and yet somehow they'd made it work so far. Along with having me attracted to them and already succumbed to my urges with two of them. I don't regret a single thing. Life was too short to not take what I wanted when it offered itself.

The only one who wasn't directly involved yet was Logan. As inconceivable as the whole thing really was, I couldn't help wondering if I'd be able to, um, *connect* with Logan in the same way. I liked to think that he and I had a different sort of affinity, a little more profound. He was the one who didn't mind baring some of his soul when we talked. He didn't walk around behind a shield of arrogance.

Orion and Seth I would happily have slept with again out of pure pleasure and getting to know them better as I felt they showed more of their real selves when in the clutches of desire. I almost laughed at myself with that thought. But Logan I wanted to get to know better emotionally. And I was genuinely looking forward to getting that chance.

Assuming he even showed up later at the crime scene.

I wandered along downtown Anchorage, and the farther I went into the residential area, the quieter the streets grew. Smoke billowed from chimneys, kids crying in houses I passed, the television loud enough to hear the game show one family watched.

At the next corner, I swung right where lofty trees lining the streets stood heavy with snow. Lamp posts lit up the sidewalk, and I moved faster to keep warm, figuring I might as well make my way toward the edge of the woods where I'd meet Logan at the crime scene.

A sudden scream had me flinching, my gaze lifting to several houses up ahead. I rushed closer, only for it to be followed up by laughing from inside.

I groaned with frustration at the lack of vamps and tuned into my ability once more. I took a deep breath to calm myself, then the energy flowed. My body vibrated like I was a struck tuning fork.

Except, there was not a single sensation of any vamps nearby. Not a goddamn thing.

It was as though all the vampires had withdrawn. Usually, I sensed them here and there, but now nothing. Were they having the weekly vampire neighborhood meeting? I laughed to myself and hurried toward the explosion of snow covered forest at the end of this street.

I had my doubts as I made my way to the meeting spot with Logan. By the time I stepped off the side of the road to head into the woods, it seemed safer to bet he wouldn't make an appearance. I retraced my steps from two nights earlier, eyes and ears open to the surrounding night. The crisp air raked its fingers through my hair and along my neck.

Then I saw him standing in the exact spot we had promised to meet. He was silent and still, looking through the heavily shadowed tree trunks into the clearing beyond. For some reason I couldn't quite pinpoint, I hesitated, just watching him.

"You're here," I said finally as I walked up.

He glanced at me. "Yeah. Are you ready?"

That was, I was learning, very much like Logan. No preamble, no wasting time, no beating around the bush. We were both there to do a job, first and foremost. His dispassionate commitment to maximum efficiency was something I ought to admire. But I couldn't deny the pang of disappointment that settled in my chest.

Had I really been hoping he might try and

seduce me? Clearly, my priorities needed to be reexamined.

I shook my head to reset my thoughts. "Okay. Let's go."

Logan's gaze lingered on me for a moment or two, as if he wasn't sure I meant what I said. I refused to acknowledge him further, and he eventually stepped out from the tree line. The tape still clung in a yellow line to the perimeter, but it was wet and sagging from two nights of half frozen rain. The clearing itself sparkled with crystal droplets that soaked through my shins as I waded toward the center.

The bodies weren't there anymore, having been carted away for examination by the coroner. In some places, I could still pick out where torsos and limbs had left imprints in bloodstained grass. The ethereal stain of violence marred every inch of this quiet clearing—the silent mark of a ruthless predator.

There was no sign of the officers who had swarmed the vicinity on the night of the killings. Except for the yellow tape and the mess of bent grass and boot prints in the soggy ground, the area might as well have been abandoned. Mildly shocking, given what had transpired here, but understandable. I knew as well as anyone that this was not a case for mortal cops to solve.

Unfortunately, it wasn't shaping up to be all that easy for me, either. The energy swirling in the air was like nothing I had ever encountered before, and nothing I found on the empty site of its trans-gressions gave me any further clues to its identity. Stumped, I stopped in my tracks and appealed to Logan for help.

The scary part was that based on Logan's surprise about this gruesome scene earlier, I doubted Orion and his men knew anything about what was killing humans. That part terrified me because if I could see a monster, I could deal with it.

An invisible enemy was lethal.

"Didn't you say you had something for this?" I asked Logan.

He regarded me evenly. I had the distinct impression that he found my confusion amusing. "I can help," he agreed. "But it's going to be a matter of personal trust."

I gave him a skeptical look. "As in, I have to trust you? I thought I was already doing that." I shrugged, holding out my hands. "That's why I'm here."

Logan dropped his gaze for an instant. He stood motionless, lost in thought. Then, at the same time I took a step toward him, he grabbed my hand and pulled me in. One lean, strong arm wrapped around my waist.

"If you say so." His lips were on mine before I could truly say anything.

*Is this real life?* My thoughts scattered in a million directions, head spinning. The love quadrangle thing had been an amusing idea, too preposterous for reality. Nonetheless, here we were, embracing like star-crossed lovers or something. In the middle of a violent crime scene, no less!

But that was where I drew the line. If he tried to get a home run right here, right now, I'd shut it down and lock the building. As it was, he might not escape a verbal lashing. Hot as he was, I hadn't shown up to have a makeout session.

The minute I opened my eyes, however, I forgot everything I was just about to say. It was like the world had been desaturated while I wasn't looking, veiled over with shades that were more light and shadow than color. I turned to Logan, and he was *glowing.* I flinched at his appearance... it freaked me out.

"What happened?" I pushed hard on his chest. "What did you do?"

He eased up just enough to get me to stop struggling. "You're fine. You can talk to them now. Look."

"What?" I forced myself to focus. He pointed toward the spot where the majority of the bodies had lain, and I gasped. A small crowd of bright, ghostly figures stood in the grass, watching us. Their faces were uncanny, features blurred and indistinct. I felt my body snap into fight or flight mode—and so did Logan, because he finally let go.

"Relax," he said flatly. "They're just spirits. If you want information, go get it." Having said his piece, he withdrew and put his hands in his pockets. I stared between him and the ghosts, dumbfounded.

"*This* is what happens when you kiss people?"

Logan shrugged. "Sometimes. And it doesn't last forever, so hurry up." He nodded toward the silent observers. "They're waiting for you."

I frowned. "Okay, but we're going to talk about this later."

"The clock is ticking," he said.

The spirits shifted restlessly as I approached them. The eye sockets on their blank faces were empty and heavily shadowed. I could barely make out noses and mouths. A couple had flowing, ethereal hair. I paused. Would they answer if I spoke to them?

There was no time to waste worrying about it. Although Logan hadn't specified a time frame, the pressure mounted steadily. Five feet away from the nearest ghost, I stopped. It pivoted toward me, its movements eerily mechanical.

"Were you killed here two nights ago?" I asked. The question seemed to grab the attention of the others, and before I knew it, they had crowded around me. The air chilled by about ten degrees. I tried to look for Logan, but the spirits blocked my view.

One of them attempted to speak. A dark void opened up on its countenance, morphing and changing with each garbled word.

"Yes," it mumbled. "I am...sad."

"I'm sorry to hear that." I took a deep breath and did my best to calm the tension in my nerves. Pure instinct had me prepped for the worst; I'd heard tales of ghosts looking to reclaim the souls of the living and things like that. What if the rest were angry rather than sad? Or spiteful? "I want to help you," I added, "but I need you to tell me what you know. Did you see who caused your death? Any of you?"

A low murmur made its way around the circle.

"I was the first," declared a different ghost. "But I only saw a large shadow behind me. It happened…too fast."

My heart started to sink a little as I saw a ripple of agreeing nods. So, whatever it had been, there was only one monster and could be anything kind of creature in reality. Many beasts hunted alone.

"All I saw…were the dead," said the next specter gloomily. "Fresh corpses…lined up so neatly." It paused, apparently thinking. "And then…I became one of them."

"Nothing?" I gazed in a slow circle at each androgynous face. "None of you saw a single thing that could help identify a murderer? What it looked like? Did it make any sounds?"

They shook their heads in unison. "Death is… funny. Our memories…like fog in rain."

*It's been two days!* I wanted to grab their noncorporeal shoulders and shake them. But already, I could feel whatever sense Logan had given me was beginning to fade. The ghosts flickered unsteadily. They started to back away. Within moments, they were completely gone, and colors were seeping back into the world.

I ran back to Logan. "No good. Any way I could get an extension?" He gazed down at me as if he'd spent the last few minutes under heavy hypnosis. "Hello? Logan? Can you do that again?"

"What? Kiss you?" He ran his finger underneath my chin, stroking my bottom lip with his thumb. "I guess so, if you wanted."

I rolled my eyes. "What I want is to see dead people for like five more minutes. Yes or no?" The second kiss was a welcome fringe benefit, but I wasn't about to let him know that.

"Let's find out." This time, he held my face in his hands and unexpectedly kissed me so deeply I was almost lifted off my feet. The sparks that shot from my lips to my toes were pure electricity. I tingled all over.

Nothing else happened. The forest was the same afterward, if a little hazy. We stared at each other.

"Damn." The word came out soft and awestruck. "It didn't work."

"Then it won't, for a while." Logan gave up a small, apologetic smile. "Sorry."

"I mean..." I chewed my lip. "Maybe there's a

placebo effect?" Instead of waiting for him to respond, I stood on my toes and kissed him once more. He drew my body close against his. The intrinsic coolness of his energy slowly turned to low heat.

There was no placebo effect, as it turned out. But I didn't pull away as his hands moved to explore. And I didn't stop him.

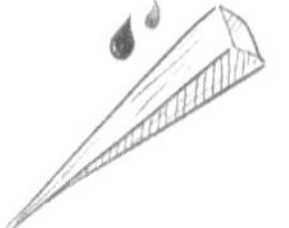

I had known from the start that Veronica was not about to be an easy conquest—that was part of her appeal. But the reality of not being able to access her whenever I wanted needled at me, especially with the thought of sharing her. That still sat on my mind like a mountain. Where was she? What was she doing? Who was she with?

That last unknown was the worst.

When the knock came at the door, I practically flew to answer it, craving a distraction from my own one-track mind. But the face that greeted me wasn't any better than Veronica's maddening beauty. The vamp sneered at me, his thin lip curling over jagged teeth. "Good evening, Clanmaster." The words had a mocking lilt that I did not like at all.

"What do you want? Out with it." I didn't bother asking him inside; whatever business he had could be conducted here in the twilight.

He glanced around, shifty eyes darting back and forth. "I've been sent to deliver a message on behalf of all my brethren." The lips pulled back into a sickly grin. "We've stumbled upon something of yours. I believe you call him Seth."

I clenched my jaw hard. "Is he dead? He must be, to have gotten captured by the likes of you."

The vamp giggled with macabre delight. "Oh, no, no. He is very much alive. And angry." The grin dropped into a split second of worry. "We'd like to return him to you as soon as possible, frankly." Regathering his composure, he cleared his throat. "So, your *honorable* presence is being requested for the purpose of negotiations. You may come alone, or bring your…associate."

The mention of Logan, however indirect, made him nervous. He took another quick look around and shifted his feet.

"What's stopping me from rolling up and putting an end to this entire charade?" I asked. My voice stayed calm, but inside I was boiling. I should have known better than to trust that fire-breathing idiot. His anger had compromised us all.

"With all due respect, Clanmaster…" The shit-eating grin was back. "We hardly think you'd keep the devil around if you didn't need him for *something*."

Annoyed by my inability to deny their logic, I capitulated. "Fine. Where is he?" The address was deeper into the city than usual, and I wondered at their brazenness. Hiding in plain sight. "Tell them I won't be long, and they'd better not waste any more of my time." Without further ado, I stepped back and slammed the door.

Had Seth been standing in front of me, I might have wrung his neck, snapped it, and throttled him again. This was far from his first blunder, but absolutely his most serious. The repercussions would have to be severe.

After I got him back, of course. I closed my eyes and sent a summons out into the world, intended for Logan.

"Seth got caught. Convene immediately at my location. Recovery operation."

Typically, it took him no longer than seconds to reply, but Logan wasn't in the mood to acknowledge me either. From him, a certain measure of aloofness was expected, and yet his coldness only blackened my mood further. Perhaps there was something in the air tonight, some golden, tantalizing whiff of mutiny.

Not that insubordination mattered so much at the moment. I had bigger problems on my hands. If Logan chose not to show up entirely, he'd regret it.

I arrived downtown in record time, brimming with utter dissatisfaction. Everyone I passed on the street gave me a double-wide berth. Haunted whispers followed my every step. This sort of passive intimidation was one of the greatest assets of a vampire's nature. A weapon I desired Veronica to hone to its sharpest edge.

Seth's prison turned out to be a semi-derelict warehouse, all but abandoned by its former owners at the edge of the city's heart. Several of its windows were boarded up or broken; the front doors stood ominously open like the slack mouth of a dead man. I showed no hesitation in striding through them, straight into the pitch dark.

"Bold as usual, I see." The voice was low and silky, gliding through the air like water. I searched in the shadows for its owner and found the glowing circles of a vampire's pale irises trained on me, unblinking. He stepped into the weak spill of light from one of the windows, and I saw the contours of a gaunt, cruel face, long and hard like a jackal's. The pallor of his skin contrasted with the intensity of his gaze.

How old was he? And how long had it been since I'd last encountered a vampire near my age? I held his stare.

"Where is the demon? Show him to me."

The vampire smiled. "As you wish." Someone flipped an invisible switch, and a light blazed on in the far back of the room. Seth sat propped against the bare concrete, affixed to the wall by thick iron chains. The cuts and bruises in stark relief on his face and body confirmed that he had not submitted quietly. He squinted at me through the sudden brightness, his expression contorted into a glowering mask.

My stomach turned. He was mine and when we fought that was what we did, but to have anyone else harm him seared through me like hot pokers. Seth was under my protection, part of my tribe. I turned back to his captor. "Your terms?" I sneered.

"Well…" The vampire cast his eyes to the side. The hairs rose on the back of my neck. Belatedly, I wondered if I had fallen into a trap. "Firstly, I would like you to know that I am not alone in this." He gestured, and a veritable army emerged from the shadows—including many of my own people. Fire burned through my veins.

"What kind of reckoning is this?" I hissed. "You think you can make your leader bow?"

"No, Clanmaster." A small contingent of Alaskans stepped forward to face me. "Hear us out before passing your judgment." They paused, glancing at each other for courage. "We want the demon to leave our territory."

"I'm listening," I grumbled. "For now." Admittedly, it was an idea that appealed to me as well for a plethora of reasons.

"He's reckless," they continued. "He's unpredictable, and he shows no loyalty to anyone other than you. He could tear this city apart if he were ever to go unchecked."

"And what makes you think that will happen?" I demanded.

"What makes them think it won't?" The vampire who had met me cut in smoothly, redirecting my rising temper toward himself. "With all due respect, Clanmaster, your iron grip on the territory is weakening. We *are* occupying you, after all." He smiled, as if he'd made a harmless little joke.

"Let it be said that your welcome is fast running out," I answered.

"Then allow me to propose a solution." He folded his hands, steepling the tips of his fingers, and smiled. "We will relieve you of this hellish burden, take him back with us, and consider a truce brokered."

"No." I didn't even have to think about it. Like hell was I ever going to give up a mercenary, no matter how frustrating and bullish he could be. I didn't give up on one of my own. That was just a needless advantage for them.

"Not even a counter-offer?" The city vamp raised his eyebrows. "You aren't much of a businessman, are you, Orion?"

"Maybe I would be if you posed more of a threat." I shook my head. "No. You have finally missed a step. This dance we've been doing is over." I held his eyes. "Get your cronies and get out. Now!"

"And what if we refuse?" came the reply.

I bared my teeth. "Then I'd be happy to assist you."

One of the lackies from the enemy clan lunged

at me, followed by others. Those loyal to me were quick to remember who their clanmaster was and took their side alongside me to fight.

I lashed out and grabbed the oncoming attacker by the neck, twisted it with ease and tossed him aside. Then I threw myself into battle, eager to spill blood and break bodies. Punching my fist right into another's chest, I kicked him aside and turned to two others. Fury licked at my insides, and with everything of late, I craved to destroy all those who stood in my way.

The battle grew brutal, and I threw punches, headbutted the enemy, and I wasn't below ripping out hearts. Blood splashed on my face as I tore out a vamp's throat, and I reveled in it.

One slammed into my back, an arm latched around my throat. I swung an arm over my shoulder and loped it over his head. I crouched forward suddenly and wrenched the asshole forward as he lost his footing, then I made quick work of snapping his neck. Shoving him off my back, I straightened and glanced to the back of the warehouse, the chains binding Seth grated heavily across the floor, igniting showers of sparks. The demon strained against his shackles. He couldn't stand to sit by and watch volley after volley of frenzied blows fly back and forth. To be denied even a small sliver of the excitement was worse than any torture for him.

But Seth's strength had been spent during the futile struggle to avoid captivity, and now he stood no chance of an unaided escape. He watched, his anger rising, as the vampire clans tore into each other. Shrieks of fury and pain echoed off the walls.

I was too preoccupied with the onslaught of enemies to spare him too much more attention. Had I been able to, I would have loosed him from his chains with my own hands so he could take his place by my side. As it was, the urban rats purported to overwhelm me. I lost sight of Seth in the ensuing frenzy.

Perhaps fittingly, my thoughts were consumed with someone else.

*Logan, where the fuck are you?*

# CHAPTER 27

VERONICA

*L*ogan had me up against a tree, my legs around his waist, arms encircling his neck.

Immediately, the rough bark of the trunk bit into my back and shoulders through my clothes. I felt my skin and clothes threaten to tear with the slightest friction.

"Wait." I tore away from his kiss breathlessly. "I can't do it like this. The tree will shred me."

Half of me expected him to shrug it off and keep going. I could feel his hardness pressing between my legs after all. To my surprise, he paused long enough to lift me away from the trunk and wrap his huge black wings around my body. The feathers were cool and soft. I sank gratefully into them.

"Better?" he murmured.

"Yeah." I ran my fingers up into his shoulder-length hair and pressed my mouth urgently to his. "Thanks."

He responded by cupping a breast and pinching my hardened nipple through the fabric of my top and bra. I moaned against his lips, lifted my hips to grind myself against him. The way in which we were positioned made it easy to be as close to him as possible; every muscle in his body seemed to ripple against me.

I dug my fingers into his back and shoulders, savoring the intense, unyielding pleasure. Logan's grip tightened on the back of my thighs. He kissed me until I couldn't breathe. My back arched against the tree trunk. The moan that left my throat turned into a kind of carnal growl.

His mouth caressed my neck greedily. The tremor of his arousal traveled all the way through to the tips of his wings. The feathers flared around me. For a moment, we were wrapped up entirely in each other. We'd only kissed, but I knew if we didn't stop, this would end up leading into something else completely.

I broke from our kiss, needing to remember my

mission and not the desire I couldn't shake. "Maybe we shouldn't do this."

Then he was letting me down carefully onto legs that were still shaking. I clung to him and laughed sheepishly. "I didn't mean for that to happen."

"Do you regret it?" He brushed the hair from my eyes.

I looked up at him and noticed that it had started to snow, very lightly. Delicate crystals adorned his ash-gray hair and eyelashes. I let myself sink into those ice blue eyes and how incredibly gorgeous Logan was. But there was so much more to him than he allowed me to see.

"No." I told the truth.

Logan smiled, then frowned. His demeanor changed completely. "Orion is calling."

I sighed. "Of course he is." I pulled out my phone to check it. Surprise—a bunch of messages from everyone's favorite clanmaster. "He tried to get in touch with me too…"

"Seth is in trouble." Logan spoke dispassionately, but I heard the resignation in his words. "We need to recover him."

"That makes it sound like he's dead," I said, unable to hide my alarm.

Logan showed no emotion. "Maybe he is."

———

Logan traced Orion to the outer edge of downtown. The place looked abandoned, a squatter's dream hovel. On the approach, we could already see a whirlwind of activity inside. "What the fuck is going on in there?" I muttered, mostly to myself.

"Let's go." Logan broke into a full run and sprinted straight for the doors. I kept hot on his heels. My trusty knife hung in its permanent place on my belt, but the closer we got, the more serious things appeared to be. My dire assessment was only confirmed when a body came smashing through one of the windowpanes. I dodged just in time to watch it hit the ground and sprawl grotesquely, held up at an awkward angle by the jagged end of an improvised stake.

"Yeah, okay. Some shit is really going down." I leaned into my run, reaching for a palm-sized silver cylinder hanging next to my pocket. "Time to bring out the big guns."

Inside, the warehouse was a chaotic mess. Vampires ripped at each other in the near-total darkness, snarling, hissing, shrieking. I saw thatches of hair and skin littered around the floor, even severed limbs and chunks of bone. *You know, I thought, in case I forgot they were fucking monsters.*

Logan darted into the chaos.

As soon as the vamps smelled living blood, a group turned toward me and came in a maddening rush. My skin crawled, but I pressed a button on the side of my metal staff, and it telescoped neatly into a staff. I intended to put it through its paces and prayed I hadn't gotten too rusty with this weapon. I cut a clean swing at the coming assault. I admired the trueness of its strikes, and I struck several in one go. Then I swung around and jabbed one end into a fiend with wild black hair. The vampire dropped dead, a hole through his undead heart. In seconds, another followed suit. Then another. I stabbed three more, and whacked another in the head hard enough to knock him off his feet.

Boots slapped the concrete floor, closer and closer they came.

One of them snatched my shirt from behind me and heaved.

"Bastard," I growled and threw my elbow into his face, dislodging him from me.

I fought, everything becoming one big blur, which came with such a crowd, with being outnumbered. This wasn't what I expected. I couldn't see Logan from the crowd of vampires encroaching.

And then someone grabbed me by the hair and yanked backward. I stumbled on my feet, the searing pain through my scalp made me cry out in shock. An icy chill raced down my spine.

I kicked and punched at everything, trying desperately to get free. The last thing I needed was to get dragged down off my feet into a death orgy of these guys.

The hand brutally pulled my head viciously downward.

I cried out but lashed outward with my staff, my other hand retrieving the stake at my belt and I struck something hard enough to elicit a grunt of pain. I wound up and took a strike, and another, while kicking. Fear bucked inside me but the numbers around me had thinned, and I would finish them.

"Fresh blood," the vampire tugging on my hair behind me said, and I flinched at the venom in his voice.

His fingers in my hair abruptly relaxed. I pulled

free and slammed my stake into the heart of a huge bastard who lunged at me. I shoved him off me, and he fell to the ground with most of the others. The few that remained seemed to recoil now.

Behind me, I heard a snap and a soft tearing sound.

The next hands that touched me were strong and familiar. I whipped around to see his face, my heart in my throat. "Orion!"

He gave me a quick inspection. "Are you hurt?"

I rubbed the back of my head. "No, I'm fine. What—"

He put his fingers to my lips. "Not now. Go find Seth, and I won't ask you why you're here." The firm, almost paternal way he said that made a flame flicker inside me, but I pushed it down. He was right. *Not now.*

"Have you seen him?" I asked.

Orion pointed, just before a new assailant attempted to leap onto his back. I pulled away as quickly as possible and began to beat my way through the pandemonium. I sliced my way through the mess, hard to tell half the time which vampire was on Orion's side. But those who stood in my way, I lashed out at.

A direct hit to the side of my face had me staggering sideways, the pain cutting along my cheek-bone. I snapped around and without thought, thrust out my stake into the monster. I caught him right in the throat, blood spurting out. He gurgled, eyes wide with shock at my retaliation as he stumbled.

"Oops. Wrong spot." I wrenched the weapon back, and in a heartbeat, thrust it directly for his heart.

Slammed in there, I smirked. "There you go, all good now."

The moment any sign of life evaporated from his eyes and he started to fall, I pulled free my stake and kept going across the warehouse.

Soon, my staff was filthy, slick with the aftermath of killing undead.

By the time I pushed through the back of the fight, I looked like I had fought my way through a warzone. My shirt and jeans had been torn in several places, and I thought I could feel the sticky trickle of blood mixing with sweat. The adrenaline pumping through my veins doubled when I laid eyes on an incredibly angry hell-demon railing against the largest set of chains I'd ever seen.

A tremor jolted through my body, and under the rush of adrenaline came pity at seeing Seth in this state. It pained me to watch him fight for escape. Every inch of me screamed to save him.

"Seth!" I ran toward him. He looked at me, the haze of rage clearing as I met his eyes. Everything else fell away as I choked on the dread splashed across his face. Nothing scared Seth, yet seeing him this panicked left me trembling.

I was suffocating.

Gasping for air to see him like this.

"Seth!" I cried out.

His expression twisted with agony.

But I had only taken a few steps before I knew something was wrong. The heat pouring off of him rivaled a nuclear reactor in crisis. His veins glowed iridescent through the reddish tan of his skin. I stopped short as the light began to pour from his eyes, mouth, even his nose.

"Oh, shit," I whispered.

"Veronica, stay away from me," he begged, his voice more scared than threatening.

A split second later, Seth erupted. That was the best way to describe it. I caught little more than a glimpse of his body shaking violently, panic scribbled over his face. His body stiffened, his shock palpable by the force of his expelling energy.

My stomach dropped through me as fear

collided into me. I knew then, something bad had happened to Seth. Something so horrendous, that it terrified him.

Then in a flash, everything disappeared in a white explosion. Sparks danced in front of my eyes, blinding me for seconds.

The shockwave that came next crashed into me, throwing me to the ground. I covered my head, curling in on myself, part of me wandering if he'd bring down the whole warehouse. Moments later, I opened my eyes to see the warehouse ceiling above me remained intact, and a tangled mess of confused vampires all still scrambling to regain the upper hand. Frantically, I glanced over to the wall where Seth had been fixed into the wall. The chains were still there, but their heavy black links lay scorched and empty. There was no sign of Seth. He'd simply vanished into thin air.

My chest tightened and I reached out a hand, a chill encasing me. "Seth?" I whispered.

Footsteps pounded toward me across the concrete floor, and Orion grabbed me by the arms, lifting me to my feet. "Are you alright?" he asked.

I shoved him as far away as he would allow. "I'm okay. But Seth is…" We both looked back to the wall. I took a slow breath in. "The fuck?" Coldness licked over my skin as worry made me sick to my stomach.

"Fuck." Orion grimaced, and a wave of worry washed over his face. Despite all their shit, he truly cared for losing his friend. "Where the hell did he go?" Fear gripped his voice.

No sooner had I come to realize how much harder this has hit Orion than I ever suspected, than a hand fell onto his shoulder from behind. I backed off as Orion turned around to face his newest challenger. There was something oddly familiar about this vamp, but it wasn't until I got a good look at his face that I realized I'd seen him before—in Seattle, coming and going around the vamp gangs' favorite haunts.

Didn't know his name, but I didn't have to. All I knew was that the guy was a prick. And apparently, Orion thought so too.

Now I had seen plenty of vamp-on-vamp infighting in Seattle; pretty much the only thing they fought was each other. And I rarely got involved. If they wanted to thin their numbers, I let them. But this was different. Orion didn't engage the way I was accustomed to seeing vampires moving. The ones back in the city had become somewhat tamed by their modern, urban surroundings. They had less of a connection to the wild, bestial part of their nature. It was like fighting suped-up humans.

Orion tapped into a much more ferocious, animalistic style. He moved almost catlike, low to the ground, each motion executed with deadly precision. His eyes never left his opponent for a second. I watched him scan for weak points as he waited for the opportune moment to strike. The Seattle vamps could be deadly in their own right, but something told me this one wouldn't stand half a chance against Orion.

Orion was like nothing I had ever seen. The air hummed with his concentrated power. I felt him coiling to attack. And when he sprang at last, it seemed I barely saw it. Just a flash of darkness and death. The city vamp sidestepped nimbly, but not quite in time. Orion caught his shoulder, leaving behind a heavy tear through clothes and flesh. Orion pivoted and attacked, bringing with him his full force. He moved so fast, I struggled to make sense of what was happening. The enemy shrieked and blood splattered to the ground. Soon followed by the vamp.

That was the beginning of the end. As I suspected, the Seattle vampire was ill-prepared to handle a "wild" creature like Orion. He was never given a chance to react properly. His jacket and shirt were shredded to rags, to say nothing of the skin beneath them. When he fell, the weak light glanced off an exposed bit of bone.

Orion pinned the enemy under his knee, glaring down into his eyes. "This act of disrespect," he growled, "will be the last thing you ever do." Without looking up, he reached his hand out toward me, palm open.

He wanted the metal staff. And I knew exactly what for.

I threw it to him.

Orion raised the weapon with one hand, the pointy end aimed to his enemy. In a flash, he struck down hard and fast. The sound of the vampire's last breath rushing from his lungs filled the whole space. His arms and legs went limp, and his head lolled to the side, eyes open and rapidly dulling. Orion didn't move until he was sure the guy was dead.

"Thank you, Veronica," he said quietly.

"I'm really worried about Seth," I admitted.

"I can tell. I'll find Seth, no matter what it takes. And you're a lot stronger than I initially thought." He put the staff into my hand, turned my face up, and kissed me. I couldn't stop myself from melting a little.

"Gross," I told him. "You smell like dead vamp."

"I'm not the only one who needs a shower," he fired back. His expression quickly sobered. "Come home with me. We don't have much time."

Behind him, the window showed a horizon just starting to lighten toward dawn. But I couldn't leave yet. "What about Logan? And…" I turned to look at the wall with the chains, unable to stop the ache growing in my chest at Seth taken. "He's not dead, is he?"

"Logan will be fine," Orion said coolly. "As for Seth…Demons don't die that easily. He annoyed the shit out of me, but I never wanted him hurt. I'll track him down one way or another, I give you my word." He took me by the hand, and while he didn't say it, I saw the worry in his eyes that maybe Seth was in more danger than he let on, and it troubled Orion. "We have to go, Veronica. Unless you want to keep me on the mantle in an urn."

I hated leaving the warehouse without any sense of where Seth was or what had happened. Fragments of pain struck through my chest at the possibility that he might be in horrible danger. The brief image of him disintegrating into light was seared into the back of my mind. I shouldn't care, and the one time we shared was just that… a one off. Yet I never wanted to see him hurt or killed, no matter how much of an ass he was. One last time, I scanned the scorched wall where he'd been earlier, my hands trembling. Anger and guilt floated to the surface. And with it came something feral surging through me that I never got a chance to help Seth. Goosebumps danced along my arms.

I twisted away, my emotions melting into one another, until they sat like a knot in my chest. This wasn't how I should feel about a demon, yet there I was feeling empty at the loss.

It was only a mild consolation to see Logan emerge from the front of the building, wings folded on his back, looking no worse for wear. He nodded to Orion. The majority of the enemy vampires had run or lay on the floor. The ones that remained bowed their heads at Orion.

"Seth is gone," Orion said softly.

Logan's brows pulled together, and he lowered his gaze momentarily as though he experienced his own moment of loss. "We need to find him." The darkness in his voice surprised me.

"We will," Orion answered curtly, and the

hunger for revenge rose in his tone. "I'll destroy anyone who stands in my way."

"And I'll help," I added.

The smile from both Orion and Logan brought with it a strange union I felt with them, with us being a team, working toward one goal.

While I swallowed the lump in my throat at Seth being gone, as a demon was he really gone somewhere else or just to hell? Whatever had been done to him had to involve a summoning or a curse. Didn't it? Or he self-combusted from rage? God, I didn't know, but I had to find out. I had only spent a short time with him, but I wasn't ready to just watch him vanish as though he never existed.

Dawn broke as we walked through the huge open room toward the door. Orion ducked behind a support pillar, covering his skin. Logan and I glanced around at the corpses of the fallen as they turned to ash, slowly at first as the sunlight found them through the windows and door, and then rapidly. A hard breeze swept through the broken windows and bore most of the ashes away.

Orion reemerged, now safely obscured by remaining in the shadows, his hood over his head, his body covered.

"What's next?" I wondered out loud. In the wake of this massive destruction, the investigation I had taken on was a favor to an old friend, now seemed too large to truly comprehend. We were standing at the tip of an iceberg whose shadow loomed deep underwater. There was something strange and mystical about this untamed northern city, this frozen, lonely place. A killer taking out innocents that I couldn't help but think it wasn't vampire or shifter related. Then there was the warring battle between the Seattle clanmaster and Orion.

With Seth gone, I had to find him. As crazy as it sounded, that ache in my chest from seeing him vanish deepened. What the hell happened to him?

Which brought me to my final dilemma…my attraction to these men. Somewhere along the way, the whole slayer and monsters being enemies had turned on its head. I had to correct that.

"The word will travel fast that the Seattle detachment is dead," Orion answered solemnly. "We will need to prepare for the worst—all of us. Because when it reaches home…" He turned his gaze to me, staring defiantly. "A storm is coming."

Yet my thoughts kept swinging back to the odd energy I'd sensed at the gruesome scene of all those butchered humans. Something was really wrong here beyond all the other shit. A darkness slid through the shadows undetected in Anchorage, and everything was about to get a whole lot worse very soon if I didn't find out who was hunting humans.

I had come to Anchorage to stop a war amid vampires. But instead, I found myself dragged into a battle zone.

And I had no plans to walk away.

THANK YOU

**They call me an outcast, weak.**
I've fought my whole life for survival, running from an attack on my family I ended up hiding with the Ash Wolves. This one move might be my biggest mistake of all. And I'm the queen of mistakes…

I let them believe I'm broken, let them believe the lies. I let them believe anything they want…as long as it isn't the truth.
There's a monster inside me, one made of teeth and claws and terrifying need. I swallow it down, hiding under the pretense of being normal. But I'm not normal. I'm anything but.
Bonding is the only thing that will save us—me and the Ash pack. Only I need someone strong enough to fight the darkness inside me…and savage enough to stay.
Will the three ruthless alphas help me…when they find out the truth of what I am?
**Shadowlands Sector is book 1 in a shifter paranormal romance story for those who love**

## Prologue
## Meira

The creak of the door alerts me to someone entering my room.

"Mama?" I roll over in bed expectedly.

But it's Jaine, our neighbor. She rushes to me with wild hazel eyes and messy blonde hair, still in her blue nightgown with patches. Her face is pale, her breaths shallow and raspy. I remember the blood and tears drenching her cheeks when she first came to our settlement after the Shadow Monsters killed her family. It still scares me to remember the fear on her face... and now, she has the same look as she hurries into my room.

The hairs on the back of my neck lift, and I draw my blanket to my chest, a whimper falling from my lips. "What's going on?"

"Meira, sweetie," she whispers, breathing heavily. She is a bit younger than Mama, but already looks out for me. "Death stalks the day. We must be swift and silent now." She chokes on her fast words as tears thread down her cheeks. There's a glint in Jaine's eyes, a window revealing a glimpse of her wolf lingering just below the surface. Her fear thickens the air in my room.

I shuffle to sit upright in bed, straightening my shoulders. "Where is Mama?" The morning light drenches my small room, and silhouettes darting past my windows outside. Their shadows are a frightening puppet show playing out across my drawn curtains.

They move fast.

There are too many of them. We're made up of a dozen females hiding in this settlement from the danger outside. The ten-foot metal fences lined with barbed wire have always kept them out.

"Jaine, what's going on?"

"The creatures are here." She glances over her shoulder to the ajar door. "You need to hide."

A chill fills my body. I hate the Shadow Monsters. I shiver, wrapping my arms around my pajama top and pants. We've been on the run from the creatures before, then Mama and I found this place. Our refuge. Or so I thought.

"I have to find Mama," I whisper.

But Jaine never answers me. She just snatches my arm and yanks me out of bed.

Pain flares through my limbs from the sickness I've suffered since birth. I wince as a pain, resembling claws, drags over my flesh. Mama insists it's related to my wolf side trying to come out. I'm already fourteen and still haven't experienced my first transformation. I shouldn't to be alive as a result, but Mama says I'm her miracle girl. For years we've fled the wolves who will have killed me for what I am and we joined other random female settlements to keep me safe. Mama lies to the other women and says I'm only eleven and not at puberty yet so they won't want to kill me. I'm thin and look young for my age. Up to now, we've survived.

"Let's be swift and silent, Meira. Repeat those words in your mind."

My stomach hurts so bad. My gaze swings to the windows, at the commotion outside. Someone screams, and I cringe, grasping on to Jaine's arm. Why isn't Mama coming to get me? Where's everyone else?

*This is a safe haven. This is our home.*

But Mama was wrong. The Shadow Monsters broke in like they always do.

Jaine leans down, gripping my shoulders, and looks me in the eyes. "Repeat the words: swift and silent. Over and over."

Tears well in my eyes. One year of peace. That is all we've been granted, and now the demons are at our doorstep again.

Jaine takes my wrist, and we duck low as we hurry out of my bedroom and down the hall. She quietly opens the small cupboard door in the hallway where we keep brooms and winter boots. It's where Mama made me practice hiding until I could find it blindfolded. There's a lock on the inside of the door too.

"Swift and silent, baby girl, okay?" Jaine's voice is panicked and shaky.

I stumble into the hiding spot and spin to face her. My heart pounds in my ears. "I'm scared."

An explosive crash comes from somewhere in the background, rattling the whole house. Jaine shuts the door hastily, and darkness swallows me. With shaky fingers, I draw the metal lock into place and back away until my heels hit a bucket. Huddling down in the corner amid threadbare clothing, I hug my knees.

I rock back and forth, trying not to whimper too loudly.

*Swift and silent.*

We were meant to be safe here. Mama promised me.

A woman screams in the distance, and I shudder.

Thundering growls, smashing glass, and scrambling footfalls hit the floorboards. I inhale my cries and wrap myself around my bent knees.

Shadow Monsters are in the house.

I can't breathe… They'll rip me apart.

There's a scraping sound, like something is being dragged across the floor. Then it falls deadly silent.

All I hear are my breaths, the hammering of my heart.

Shadows pass over the wood slats just outside my door. With it comes a rancid meat smell. My stomach tightens so much, I think I'm going to vomit.

I flinch as another scream pierces the air, and I bite down hard on my bottom lip to stop myself from sobbing.

Someone slams into the wall just outside my hiding place. I shove backward, my spine pressing against the wall. Every inch of me is trembling ferociously, but I don't speak. Not a sound. Or they'll hear me.

A slurping sound mangled with screams fills my ears.

I want to yell, to run. My hands plaster to my ears and I tuck my chin into my chest, rocking back and forth.

*Swift and silent.*

*Swift and silent.*

*Swift and silent.*

*Swift and silent.*

I don't know how much time passes. Tears drench my cheeks. I can't stop trembling. I finally push forward and press my ear to the door. Sweat trickles down my back. My legs are cramping from sitting so long in one spot. *Mama, where are you?*

When I get too anxious to wait anymore, I unlatch the lock. The door creaks as I push it open. My heart stops.

I freeze on the spot.

*Inhale.*

*Exhale.*

Sitting here makes me an easy target. *Swift and silent.* So I force myself to look out.

The walls look like someone splashed red paint

across them, but the sickening odor tells me it's blood.

Jaine lies on her back, her legs and arms twisted and broken. Her stomach lays splayed open. Shattered ribs poke up through the fabric of her pajamas. I'm going to be sick.

Terror bubbles on my throat.

*"Don't be afraid of death,"* Mama would say. *"Our bodies are just vessels before we ascend to heaven. If you see someone dead, just look away and keep going."*

I whip my gaze away from Jaine and scramble out of the closet.

The silence is suffocating.

Moving fast through the old house barren of furnishings, I find no one around. I rush barefoot from one room to the next. Abandoned. *Mama, where are you?* Cold sweat sticks the fabric of my pajamas to my skin.

There are other homes in this homestead she may be hiding in, so I creep outside into the yard.

Rain falls as the bruised sky rumbles with thunder. A flash of lightning plunges across the heavens.

But I gasp at the sight before me.

Bodies lie everywhere, chaos all around me. Mothers. Children. Guards. A splitting ache tears through me. I should have tried to help rather than hide. I scan familiar faces, my stomach churning from the sickness, from seeing friends and neighbors torn apart and bleeding.

I hurry from one body to the next, searching for her face. Hope flickers inside me that she made it out alive. That she found a hiding space. I pivot around, and my gaze lands on a familiar face.

"Mama!" A cry bursts from my lips, and I rush forward, dropping to my knees by her side. Blood is pouring from the deep gash across her torn throat. I can't look at the injury, so I cup her face and place mine close to hers like she'd always do to me. Our noses touch; her skin is cool against mine. Tears fall and drip onto her cheeks. Dark brown hair spreads out around her head, her skin pale, tainted with blood. Everyone always says I'm beautiful like her with sharp cheekbones, small nose with a sprinkled with freckles, and a round face. But the only similarity I see right now are the light bronze eyes I look into.

"Mama," the word escapes my lips.

My insides shatter like glass.

"Mama! *Please*. Wake up." I hold her face, my arms trembling. "Please don't leave me." I won't survive on my own. I'm completely alone.

She never responds, and I just cry at her side. Mama is all I have left in the world. My breaths billow, and I hug myself. A cold wind cuts through my hair. The rain comes down heavily now, drenching me, but I don't move.

Mama will never drag me into her arms ever again or cover my face in kisses. She'll never wake me up with tickles. Or hold me tight at night when the storms come. I feel so lost. So angry. So scared. My breaths don't come easy as my heartbroken sobs float on the air.

Mama looks so peaceful lying down, her muscles relaxed as opposed to her always being tense when she was alive. My heart gives a painful throb when a gravelly snarl grows behind me.

I jerk my head up and twist around fast. Terror reverberates through my head.

A Shadow Monster stands at the corner of the house. Lanky and thin, his torn clothes hang loosely from his bony frame. He has no lips; they've been eaten away. Only teeth, broken and stained. That's all I see at first. Then the bulging eyes from the gaunt face. He is so skinny… starved.

I scramble backward up on my feet, panic kicking me in the gut.

He lurches forward, groaning.

Retreating, I want the world to open up and swallow me.

But the creature doesn't come to me. He falls to his knees in front of a dead woman and shoves his mouth into her torn stomach, eating. That slurpy sound makes me gag.

Bile hits the back of my throat. I recoil when someone brushes against my shoulder.

Spinning, I shriek to find another undead creature inches from me. Instinct kicks in, and I back away. Hair like straw dangles over her lifeless face. My heel hits something, and I fall. Hitting the ground, I shuffle backward, noting the fleshy, gory, torn-off leg I tripped over.

Fear pummels through me as my brain numbs. I can't do this. I can't.

The creature pounces.

I yell and flinch backward.

But it dives for the dead child beside me. My heart pounds in my throat.

The Shadow Monsters didn't see me. How? It's as though I'm invisible or something.

That's who I am. Invisible. I have to believe that or I won't move.

I scramble to my feet and find someone's disembodied finger stuck on my pajama pants with so much red gung.

Nausea pulses through me.

The undead's head snaps up in my direction, eyes falling to the stain. I shove the pants down my legs and toss them aside. I recoil as the creature eyes the pajamas crumpled on the ground.

Another creature who staggers on his feet bumps into me before pushing past me. A strangled cry escapes from my lips, and I slap a hand over my mouth to silence my sobs. I back away from the river of undead coming this way through the broken fence.

God, there are so many.

Shadow Monsters were once shifters, just like me. Or maybe mere humans, or one of a number of other supernaturals in the world. Mama said the virus that destroyed our world didn't discriminate and took everyone it could, turning them into the undead.

Not one of the Shadow Monsters so much as looks my way, but they dart to the recently dead to feed. It's all they know.

My heart is beating too hard, too fast.

I don't know what's going on, but I have to get out of here before my strange luck runs out and they start noticing me. So I push past the horde of creatures.

Once clear, I run toward the main street, my feet now bare and bloody and in pain as I pound the worn path.

Jaine was right. *Swift and silent.*


**Continue Reading Shadowlands Sector here...**

**Shadowlands**

Shadowlands Sector, One
Shadowlands Sector, Two
Shadowlands Sector, Three

**Chosen Vampire Slayer**

Night Kissed
Moon Kissed
Blood Kissed

**Winter's Thorn**

To Seduce A Fae
To Tame A Fae
To Claim A Fae

**Shadow Hunters Series**

Boxed Set 1

**Wicked Heat Series**

Wicked Heat #1
Wicked Heat #2
Wicked Heat #3

**Elemental Series**

Taking Breath #1

Taking Breath #2

**Gods and Monsters**
Apollo Is Mine
Poseidon Is Mine
Ares Is Mine
Hades Is Mine

**Haven Realm Series**
Hunted (Little Red Riding Hood Retelling)
Cursed (Beauty and the Beast Retelling)
Entangled (Rapunzel Retelling)
Princess of Frost (Snow Queen)

**Kingdom of Wolves Co-write with C.R. Jane**
Wild Moon

**Playing with Hellfire Co-write with Harper A. Brooks**
Playing with Hellfire
Hell in a Handbasket

**Thief of Hearts Series Co-write with C.R. Jane**
Siren Condemned
Siren Sacrificed
Siren Awakened

### Broken Souls Series Co-write with C.R. Jane

School of Broken Souls

School of Broken Hearts

School of Broken Dreams

School of Broken Wings

### Fallen World Series Co-write with C.R. Jane

Bound

Broken

Betrayed

Belong

### Beautiful Beasts Academy Co-write with Kim Faulks

Manicures and Mayhem

Diamonds and Demons

Hexes and Hounds

Secrets and Shadows

Passions and Protectors

Ancients and Anarchy

Subscribe to Mila Young's Newsletter to receive exclusive content, latest updates, and giveaways. Join here.

ABOUT MILA YOUNG

Best-selling author, Mila Young tackles everything with the zeal and bravado of the fairytale heroes she grew up reading about. She slays monsters, real and imaginary, like there's no tomorrow. By day she rocks a keyboard as a marketing extraordinaire. At night she battles with her mighty pen-sword, creating fairytale retellings, and sexy ever after tales. In her spare time, she loves pretending she's a mighty warrior, walks on the beach with her dogs, cuddling up with her cats, and devouring every fantasy tale she can get her pinkies on.

Ready to read more and more from Mila Young?
Subscribe to her newsletter
www.subscribepage.com/milayoung

*For more information...*
milayoungarc@gmail.com